"I believe you're innocent.

"You had nothing to do with the murder," Aidan insisted. "But something happened to make you suspicious of anyone who comes near you. I'm warning you, Ruth. I mean to stick around until I find out what it is."

"No!" she cried. "I don't need you! I don't need anyone."

'We all need someone!"

Not me! Ruth thought about making a mad dash for her car. Would he follow her? "What do you want from me?"

"I want to kiss you," he said. "I've wanted to kiss you from the first moment I saw you."

She was truly frightened now. "Well, I don't want to kiss you!"

"Is that so? Then run away while you still can. Because I'm going to be one step behind you—all the way."

Dear Reader:

The spirit of the Silhouette Romance Homecoming Celebration lives on as each month we bring you six books by continuing stars!

And there are some wonderful stories in the stars for you. In the coming months, we're publishing romances by many of your favorite authors such as Sondra Stanford, Annette Broadrick and Brittany Young. In addition, we have some very special events planned for the summer of 1988.

In June, watch for the first book in Diana Palmer's exciting new trilogy *Long, Tall Texans*. The initial title, *Calhoun*, will be followed later by *Justin* and *Tyler*. All three books are designed to capture your heart.

Also in June is Phyllis Halldorson's *Raindance Autumn*, the second book of this wonderful author's *Raindance Duo*. Don't miss this exciting sequel!

Your response to these authors and other authors of Silhouette Romances has served as a touchstone for us, and we're pleased to bring you more books with Silhouette's distinctive medley of charm, wit and—above all—*romance*.

I hope you enjoy this book and the many stories to come. Come home to Silhouette—for always!

Sincerely,

Tara Hughes
Senior Editor
Silhouette Books

ELIZABETH HUNTER

The Tides
of Love

Silhouette *Romance*

Published by Silhouette Books New York

America's Publisher of Contemporary Romance

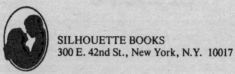

SILHOUETTE BOOKS
300 E. 42nd St., New York, N.Y. 10017

Copyright © 1988 by Elizabeth Hunter

ISBN: 0-373-08577-X

First Silhouette Books printing May 1988

Printed in the U.S.A.

Books by Elizabeth Hunter

Silhouette Romance

ELIZABETH HUNTER

uses the world as her backdrop. She paints with broad and colorful strokes; yet she is meticulous in her eye for detail. Well-known for her warm understanding of her characters, she is internationally beloved by her loyal and enthusiastic readers.

Prologue

Facing Aidan Wakefield, her barrister, was as much of an ordeal for Ruth Gaynor as her first appearance in court had been. She was certainly learning the intricacies of the English legal system, although this was not the way she would have chosen to do so.

She had always known, in the way that one does know such things, that the legal profession was divided into two branches, but until she had come up against the necessity of having both a solicitor to prepare the brief and a barrister to plead her cause in court, she had never consciously thought about these things. If anything, her view of the law had been romantic, with right always triumphing over evil, and with the innocent protected from others who wanted to bring about their downfall.

Ruth had learned it wasn't like that at all. Her solicitor was inadequate; worse, she was very much afraid he had no interest in her at all. He had agreed with the police from the very beginning that it was an open-and-shut case, and the only reason he hadn't abandoned her to what he plainly considered her just deserts was that he had several times seen her on television and rather fancied having a famous client for a change. She sighed. She had been getting quite a lot of good work lately—

"And did you?" asked the barrister with a purposeful air.

She cast her tormentor a startled glance. Had she what? How awful that she hadn't been listening to him. Somewhere in the back of her mind she wondered what this man really thought of her and the miserable pass she had come to. Mr. Wakefield had a no-nonsense look about him that might have appealed to her under different circumstances. At the moment, though, Aidan Wakefield wasn't a man at all to her; he was a functionary of British justice, supposedly on her side in the battle ahead. But she wasn't sanguine about her chances. She knew that to any of the witnesses it was obvious she had killed Jonathan Ross. Only she was in a position to believe completely in her own innocence.

Ruth made a desperate effort to pull herself together, straightening her back and summoning up a weary smile that was unwise. She bit her lower lip instead to stop it from trembling. She very much hoped she was not going to burst into tears.

Aidan Wakefield was exhausted. His chambers had never dealt with this particular firm of solicitors before and, if he had anything to do with it, they never would again. The brief had been so badly prepared that he doubted anything was accurate on the closely written paper before him. Worse yet, his clerk was still arguing out the details of the solicitor's fee. The man was clearly determined to milk this actress for every penny she had. They weren't tactics Aidan could approve, but this morning he had shrugged his shoulders, trusting his clerk to work out the details in his client's best interest.

Looking at Ruth Gaynor, Aidan thought her unbelievably plain and vulnerable. Without makeup she had a clean and shiny look. He was enough of a ham himself to know, however, that a face like that was a gift from the gods for any actress. With no more than a touch of makeup she could transform herself from angel to devil and back again. It didn't mean she was either, but her face made it a great deal harder to read where her inclinations lay. He eyed her thoughtfully. The bone structure of her face was good—she would age well—and her eyes were truly magnificent.

"Did you kill him?" he repeated patiently, bringing his mind back to business.

"I don't think so," she said.

"Don't you know?" he shot at her.

She drew back a little, but her manner remained controlled. "Once upon a time I knew. It was all so simple. I saw this knife on the floor, quite close to where I was standing, and I picked it up to return it to the props department. It had blood on it."

"You knew it was blood?"

"I thought it was Kensington Gore at first."

He didn't know the allusion. She explained slowly that the red stuff they used for blood onstage was frequently referred to as Kensington Gore, after the street in London that ran along the side of Hyde Park and Kensington Gardens.

"Blood, gore, you see. Get it?"

He nodded. "When did you know it was blood—and that the events you had witnessed were real?"

"When I smelt it. Until then I'd thought the whole thing was a joke." Ruth smiled wryly. "There was this

fellow walking around until he fell to the floor. I thought
he was putting it on. I even told him that he was over-
doing the agony bit, that people didn't really die like that.
I nearly fainted when I realized that he was truly dead
and that the knife in my hand had killed him.''

The barrister pounced. "You spoke to him? You knew
him?'' He ran an eye over the relevant passage in the
brief again. "It says here you'd never set eyes on the man
before!''

"I knew of him and I may have seen him at the Marlborough Arms. A lot of would-be actors hang out in the
pub, picking up the latest gossip, hoping to hear of a part
going that they may be able to persuade a producer to let
them try for. Most of my profession are out of work most
of the time. It gets to be a way of life.''

"You don't seem to have any trouble finding work,''
Aidan said dryly. If he had hoped to get a reaction from
her, he succeeded all too well. She looked at him as
though she hated him, her large eyes full of unshed tears.

"I'm a bloody good actress, that's why! I've been
lucky, too. But I've had my share of the down side, tell
me any actress who hasn't. I've waited tables, scrubbed
floors, been patronized by the untalented, and turned
down parts I badly wanted because of the strings attached to them. Any work I've had, I've *earned* by sheer
hard work. I'd scorn to get it any other way!''

A memory of Audrey Hepburn in *My Fair Lady*,
screaming that she was a good girl, she was, came un-
bidden to his mind. He had no doubt that his client had
seen the film too, not once, but many times. He noticed
for the first time that she was rubbing a long, raw-looking
scratch on her arm.

"Heaven knows if I'll ever find work again after this!''
she said.

"You might not be available to take it," he goaded.

His words had a remarkable effect on her, he noted with interest. It was possible that this woman was innocent after all. She looked more lost than ever, a grey tinge lining her lips. He felt a rush of sympathy for her and strove to regain his usual objectivity. She was plain, unbelievably plain, he told himself. But Aidan couldn't deny she was the most attractive woman he had seen for a long, long time. Forget the fatigue, the look of hurt that threatened to undermine her professional control; forget the way she had pulled her hair back and tied it in a loose knot at the back of her neck as if she hadn't had enough energy to do anything else with it; forget the baggy, shapeless clothes she was wearing; she still had a grace of movement and an underlying sweetness that would have made her memorable in any company. And those eyes!

"How did you get that scratch on your arm?" he asked conversationally.

"I don't know." She didn't look much interested. "I don't remember doing it at all," she added defensively. "I can't imagine why not. I must have done it when I picked up the knife."

"To yourself?" He was frowning at her.

"Well, I don't know how I got it otherwise," she said, dismissing it casually. Her calm was annoying. It would do her no good to play games with him, Aidan thought. But perhaps she really didn't know how she had got the cut.

He looked at his watch. "Your solicitor should have been here half an hour ago. Did he send any message?"

A faint colour washed Ruth's pale face. "He made a pass at me," she mumbled in a mortified voice. "I told him to go. Anyway, who needs him?"

Aidan Wakefield stared at her. "You do. You can't get a barrister to appear for you except through a solicitor. If you've really sacked him you'll have to find someone else. I can't do anything for you unless you have a solicitor to brief me."

She muttered something about red tape and the whole legal profession. It was neither flattering nor careful of his feelings, but it seemed to do her good. He'd thought she had been on the verge of falling apart, but she seemed to have a better grip on herself now. Certainly she had been ill-used by the solicitor and her situation was far from pleasant. He felt an unusual stirring of sympathy for Ruth Gaynor. Aidan didn't like getting involved with his clients. It didn't make for a clear head. Years ago, he had promised himself to put his finer feelings in cold storage until he had carved out a lucrative career for himself. Women had come and gone in his life, their images lingering sometimes in his memory, but then eventually fading. He supposed he'd never been in love. This woman was different, though. Even her scent was different—she smelt of herself and soap and water, like a newly washed child, warm and cuddly. He wondered how old she was. It wouldn't be hard to find out. It had to be in the brief somewhere. "Oh well," he said aloud. "I expect I can talk him back onto the case—"

"As long as I don't have to see him again!"

Aidan tried to ignore the innocently determined pout of her mouth and bring his mind back to the matter in hand. Any other way was marked "Dangerous" and "No Entrance"—he'd be a fool if he thought otherwise. He took out a pen and began to run through the brief again.

"You are, twenty-nine, thirty years old?" he asked. She looked much younger.

"Thirty. Thirty today, as a matter of fact."

She made it sound as though it mattered no more to her than any other day. He had always taken his own birthday rather seriously, even when he was alone. Last birthday, he had baked himself a cake and iced it, solemnly eating it with a cup of tea, pretending to himself that he didn't know what the word loneliness meant.

He tried to avoid her eyes. "Unmarried?" he said in an official tone.

"Yes, unmarried. I haven't time to get married, or for affairs, either. They're messy and they interfere with one's concentration. Theatrical relationships never succeed unless one partner is prepared to sacrifice his, or her, whole career to the other. It's the same with brief affairs," she added wryly. "There are always strings attached."

Aidan couldn't believe it. He stabbed his notebook with his pen. "Many men must have found you attractive—"

"Only when I'm onstage. When I'm pretending to be someone else—correction, when I *am* being someone else—then I'm attractive. I'm invincible; the whole world lies at my feet. When I'm myself, I'm a mess. Nobody looks twice at me when I'm off stage."

He could have told her differently. There was something about that loose-limbed charm of hers that had certainly got to him. Aidan shifted uncomfortably on the hard wooden chair the prison had provided him with.

"Okay," he said. "In your own words, suppose you tell me what happened—just as you remember it, with nothing put in, and nothing left out."

"You make it sound easy," she commented. "It would be if I'd been expecting it. I think I was too shocked at finding he was really dead to remember anything else."

"You must know why you went to the pub in the first place?"

"Oh, that." Again she responded with that curious indifference. "I went to meet Jonathan Ross, the producer of the new play I'm going to be in—*was* going to be in. I'd never met him before and the whole place was crowded with theatrical people, all of them talking at the tops of their voices. We actors can't drink a glass of water without making a business out of it—you never know when somebody might be watching, and it's all good practice anyway."

Ruth was straying from the subject, but Aidan found himself enjoying it. He didn't stop her. She seemed to believe in economy of movement, he thought. If she was as uncomfortable on her chair as he was on his, her composure was a miracle. "Is that what *you* do?" he heard himself asking.

She gave the question some thought. "I do and I don't," she said at last. "The best actors are those who are sufficiently unself-conscious to observe what everyone else is doing. Usually, I can do that, because I am good. That's why it bothers me that I remember so little of where everyone was and how they looked when I realized that Jonathan Ross really was dead. At the time I thought he was a crazy young actor showing off. He seemed so terribly young—far too young to be a famous producer. He had a lost, little-boy look and was not at all the man of the world I'd expected." She broke off, wishing the words unsaid. "I was pushing my way to the bar to ask if he had arrived. I was almost there when this man began writhing around. That's when I told him he was hamming it up, that people don't die like that, screaming. I thought I knew. I've died quite often on the stage. One wants to make a tragedy of it, not a farce." Ruth came to an abrupt halt. There was nothing more to be said about that awful day. It had happened and that was all there was to it. It was the beginning of a nightmare that she hoped would end soon. Her prospects were looking better, though. The barrister, still coolly observant, seemed willing to believe her.

"Tell me about Jonathan Ross," he invited her.

"Everybody said he was brilliant. I'd never worked with him before. He saw me in a series on television and thought I'd do for his next play. It was quite a chance for me, or so my agent kept telling me. The thing was, I didn't much want to do it. I was tired, having been doing a series and a play in Birmingham at the same time. I wasn't sure I wanted to commit myself to anything else."

"Did you tell him so?"

"I didn't tell him anything. He was dead and, by the time the crowd noticed what had happened, I'd been left holding the knife. The strange thing was that his widow sent me flowers. I don't even know her."

"Hmm. Surprising. And you didn't tell the police?"

"No."

"Was there a card with them?"

"'Flowers for the dead,' it said." Ruth tried to pretend, to herself at least, that she hadn't minded receiving that cryptic note. "I heard afterward that she always sent flowers to Jon's leading ladies as a kind of warning that they wouldn't get anything else from her. From what I'd heard, he was a bit of a lad—"

"But you had no personal experience of her, er, methods?" Aidan cursed himself for the twinge of jealousy. He had no business feeling anything at all for this woman.

"No," she said, "at least I didn't have to have a battle about that." She heaved a sigh, defeated. There would be no part now that he was dead. It had been a long, long time since she had allowed herself to take time off and think about which way she wanted to go next. Well, she'd probably have all the time she needed in prison, she told herself bitterly. And then some.

Ruth saw Aidan Wakefield twice more after his meeting with her in prison, both times in the reluctant company of her wretched solicitor, who did nothing but bleat that there was no hope for her. Sadly, she had been inclined to agree. *Someone* had killed Jonathan Ross, and none of the witnesses had seen him with anyone but Ruth.

And then, suddenly, when they were almost ready to go to court, all charges against her were withdrawn, for if there was no defence, there wasn't enough hard evidence against Ruth to be sure of a conviction, either. The police threatened that they'd get the proof one day and her punishment would be that she'd never know when they'd be coming for her. *We know you're guilty,* they kept telling her. *You may think you've made fools out of us, but we'll get you in the end.*

Ruth believed them.

When her agent, Judith, came to collect her, she being the nearest person to a friend Ruth had in all the world, Ruth was so apathetic that she couldn't be bothered to discuss anything that lay in the future; Ruth genuinely believed she didn't have one. What was the point of trying out for a part if she wouldn't be free long enough to enjoy it?

Dropping her client and longtime friend at the door of her flat, Judith had eyed her speculatively. She knew that Ruth was not the sort of person to commit murder and she was worried about her. Judith thought she might still be in shock and suggested she go away for a while.

Ruth might never have seen Aidan Wakefield again if he hadn't managed to find out that her agent was the well-known Judith Tate, and taken the trouble to go to her office.

"You want to get in touch with Ruth Gaynor?" Judith had brooded while she examined the man's face, trying to make up her mind if she could trust him or not.

"Right. I was almost her barrister—" Aidan had said as genially as possible.

"And you want to see her again? Why?"

He felt at a disadvantage. "Prison changes people," he muttered, but Judith smiled at him, instantly reading his intent.

It was about time Ruth found some interest outside of work. And Judith decided she liked Aidan very much indeed. "You know you haven't a chance with her," she said brightly. "No one has. She's never had a personal life since I've known her. It's work, work, nothing but work!"

"She isn't working now," he pointed out.

Judith had stood up. "No. Well, I'm going for lunch. If you want to waste your time, Mr. Wakefield, make sure that my door is locked when you go, won't you? You're lucky. I keep my files up to date, A through to Z."

He hadn't paused to ask himself why Judith trusted him with her client's address. It was enough for him to know that she did. He wasn't quite sure how to explain why he wanted it. Aidan searched the files, feeling like a criminal, with his heart doing jerks all the time until he came to Ruth Gaynor's file. Her address was neatly typed in one corner. But beside it there was another, written in with a recent date beside it. Ruth had left London. Aidan impulsively lifted out one of the several eight-by-ten-inch photos in Ruth's file. "Well, well, Miss Ruth Gaynor, try hiding from me now—if you can!" he told the glossy picture. She looked remote and very beautiful in the photograph. She looked vulnerable, too, and he wondered if he was the first one to see this quality in her. What was she afraid of? Was there fear in that shadow he thought he saw in her eyes? He didn't know, but he meant to find out. "I'm going to learn every detail there is to know about you—and then we'll see. I can't help thinking you need me."

Aidan grinned to himself, wondering if he wasn't about to commit the cardinal sin of his profession and fall in love with his client. His *innocent* client? he wondered. *Very* innocent, he reassured himself and grinned again. Somehow he had never seen himself as a knight in shining armor before, and something told him that it was going to take all his cunning and every bit of his charm to persuade Ruth Gaynor to see him that way.

"Oh my word!" he had said out loud. "I don't know what it is about you, Ruth, but I'm sure as 'eggs is eggs' that you need help! *My* help," he added a shade self-consciously. Carefully he put the photo back in the file and shut the drawer, expelling a long breath of relief. At least he knew now where she was hiding herself—even if he didn't yet know why.

Chapter One

Ruth recognized Aidan at once. She closed her eyes in disbelief, not wanting to believe that he was actually there and undoubtedly looking for someone. She had come up here to be alone!

The only different thing about him was his clothes. Today he was dressed in a pair of pale beige trousers and a matching knit shirt that made him seem both taller and broader than she remembered him. Or perhaps that was because she was lying flat on her back and looking up at him. He came closer, standing over her.

"You're blocking out the sun," she accused him. "What are you doing here, anyway?"

Aidan didn't reply, but he noted the husky quality of her voice and the quick interest she had been unable to hide. He was certain she had felt the jolt of recognition between them, too. Thirty years old, he mused, and yet she still wanted him to believe that there had never been anyone special in her life. He hadn't believed her at first, but not even the press at the time of her arrest had been able to dig up any personal details about her. No parents, no siblings, no indiscreet friends—no nothing!

Ruth watched him sit down beside her with a grunt, easing his back against the sun-warmed stones of Hadrian's Wall. They both explored the sky with their eyes, pretending to be unaware of each other. There were small, puffy clouds, as white as the sky was blue, skidding across the horizon in front of the cold wind. At least it wasn't raining, but the sun she had referred to wasn't much in evidence, either. Ruth remembered Geordie country as always having rain, but that might have been because she had never known much happiness in the years she had lived there. It was here that she had learned, the painful way, that the only person she could rely on was herself. Others might intend to be helpful and friendly, but when it came to the crunch, they had their own families and friends. As a foster child, she had been on her own, belonging to nobody.

"So this is your home territory," he said at last. "It's very beautiful."

Ruth's eyes flickered over him, noting the tan he seemed to have acquired from nowhere—he certainly hadn't got it in England—not that year. He looked healthy and fit. He was probably at the end of his holiday, she thought with some relief. His being there probably had nothing to do with her at all.

"The boards are my home territory," she murmured.

"The stage? You must have had a childhood somewhere. Why not here?"

"Are you telling me or asking me?"

A smile flickered across his face. "Telling you. You see I know you went to school in Berwick and left at sixteen, with eight, or was it nine, O-levels to your credit. Your teachers thought of you as being university material, but you wouldn't have anything to do with it. Why not?''

She shrugged her shoulders. ''That solicitor must have prepared a better brief than I gave him credit for,'' she said sulkily. ''I should have thought you'd have forgotten all about me by now. You never even got to give your great performance, thank God!''

''Thank God indeed,'' he echoed piously. ''You'd have needed His help if you had ever come to trial. You did nothing to help your own defence, did you? I learned about your school career from other sources, as a matter of fact. Your teachers were a great deal more willing to talk about their famous ex-pupil than most other people were.''

''Don't you mean their most notorious ex-pupil?'' she corrected him wryly.

''Do I? You tell me.''

But Ruth wasn't about to tell him anything. She resented his finding out things about her that she didn't want anyone to know. Who did he think he was? She tensed up, resenting his presence beside her, resenting him for being in the neighborhood at all. Why had he come? It was still possible that he had come like any other visitor to Northumberland to see for himself the famous Roman Wall that crossed the countryside from one shore to the other. She didn't believe that, however, not for a moment. Just wanting to see the sights wouldn't begin to explain why he had been so busy, tracking her down, making enquiries about her at her old school. And what else had he done? What did he want from her? Didn't he know that she had nothing left to give anyone, that she hadn't had for a very, very long time?

''I'm not telling you anything,'' she said at last. ''You can do the telling. Tell me the story of your life, Mr. Wakefield, warts and all!''

He looked amused and pleased with himself. Perhaps he thought she really was interested. "What do you want to know?" he asked.

"What you're doing here."

"I came to see the second-most-famous wall in the world. What else?" he retorted.

"The *second* most famous?" The tartness in her voice dismayed her. It was a dead giveaway that she was a local, with all of a local's enthusiasm for the Roman wall that had been built all those many years ago to keep the Picts safely out of Roman England. Ruth had walked every inch of it; spent hours watching the archaeologists reclaiming the lives of those who had defended the southern kingdom so long ago, leaving a shoe here, a brooch there, and even some of their letters home, written on tablets of wood.

"Never heard of the Great Wall of China?" he teased her.

"Oh, *that*! I've never been to China." Oh dear, she thought, there I go again, making out that there is nowhere in the world to equal Northumberland. She hadn't realized she was so fond of the place. Yet she had always thought it was one of the most beautiful spots on earth. She loved to walk from the northeast corner to Sewingshields Crag, following the wall where it led through a wood, was lost in it for a while, and then emerged on the summit of a crag, as if playing a game of hide-and-seek. The wall brought her childhood fancies to life. Far down below, King Arthur and his knights are sleeping, and there's Hotspur and his hounds lost somewhere in a valley below the Cheviot.

If she told Aidan romantic tales like those, would he forget all the things he seemed determined to discover about her?

She could suggest they take the walk toward Steel Rigg and Twice Brewed Inn, with its view over the South Tyne Valley and the Brampton Falls, where one could follow the wall for miles, where Hadrian's Roman sentries once walked? She doubted Aidan would be interested in any of that. He looked too much of a sun lover to stay long in these parts. There was a saying in Northumberland that if one could see the Cross Fell from the inn, it was about to rain; if one couldn't, it was already raining...

"I gather you were born up here?" he remarked suddenly.

He had dropped the words into her thoughts with all the adroitness of an experienced fly fisherman.

"Probably," she replied. It was no more than the truth; she didn't know where she had been born. "Where were you born, Mr. Wakefield?"

"In Durham. My mother named me after St. Aidan. She has a fancy for our local saints, especially for St. Cuthbert because he wouldn't allow anyone to harm his favourite eider ducks. They're still sometimes known as 'Cuthbert's chicks' locally. Did you know that?"

Ruth was irritated out of all proportion that she had never heard the story before. She'd had Aidan Wakefield pegged as a Southerner, a Londoner, one of those creatures of soft living who knew nothing about anything that happened north of the Watford Gap. She wondered why she should be so sensitive about everything he said. The trouble was that she was far too aware of the attractive man seated beside her. She simply couldn't ignore him, and yet she didn't want him to come too close. He already knew far too much about her.

"If you know so much about the locality," she said sourly, "tell me what you know about Hadrian's Wall."

He sounded half-asleep when he answered, not dangerous at all. "What is there to know?" he countered.

If Ruth hadn't known better, she might have mistaken Aidan for a paper tiger, a teddy bear of a man who wanted no more from her than a brief cuddle and a little comfort. She wished she knew what had really brought him here.

She began to recite the kind of facts that anyone can read in any guidebook, uncaring if she was boring him. "It was built by the Roman legionnaires, the elite of the Roman army, every man a Roman citizen—"

"Not by the citizens of Northumberland?"

"I expect they were citizens of both, most of the builders. Not even the Roman emperors were all Romans by birth. They were all sorts. Wasn't it Trajan who was a Spaniard?"

He smiled as if to force her to admit she was enjoying his company, and she did a slow burn at the sight of it, deliberately turning her eyes away. He moved an inch or so closer. "I seem to remember that at least one of the Romans was proclaimed emperor in York."

She edged away from him. "I suppose you're here on holiday?" she asked him. "I hope you didn't expect to see much of the sun."

"Northumberland has other attractions, especially right now. And, before you tell me that I ought to be back in London, working my tail off for my clients, the mighty courts of England are on holiday just now—"

"Regardless of all those waiting in jail to come up for trial? I wonder if any of those superior judges knows how it feels to be deprived of one's freedom for maybe months, waiting for the wheels of justice to roll. And then, when your big moment finally does come, you find yourself at the mercy of some failed actor who doesn't know the first thing about you and who only wants to score points against the other side, so that everybody will say what a marvellous job he did on behalf of his client!"

"A trifle cynical," he commented.

"But there's some truth in it, isn't there?" she insisted.

"More than most of us like to admit. But then most clients are eager to reveal the relevant facts about themselves. You may yet need to be a little more forthcoming, my dear. The police haven't arrested anyone else for the murder of Jonathan Ross, but somebody killed him. Was it you?"

He could feel her withdrawal and cursed himself for being a tactless fool. If he wanted to know her better, this was the last way to go about it. First of all, he must persuade her that he was her friend. Friend? No, he wanted more than that, but he would have to start by being her friend, he thought. She could certainly do with one.

Ruth took a deep breath. "You've never been on the other side of your profession, have you? It has nothing to do with justice! Or rather society, or any of those fine ideals we're all told about. It's a game where those who play their parts well can get away with murder—" She broke off, a dry sob wrenching at her chest. "I didn't mean that precisely. I've never been so frightened in my life! You're told you're innocent; you *know* you're innocent—but they lock you up just the same! They may call it remanding you in custody, but it feels much the same as being locked up because society believes you to be guilty."

"With me for a barrister?" He tried to laugh her out of her memories. "Surely you didn't think I'd let them convict you of something you hadn't done."

She made a face at him. "Now why would I think that? You didn't believe a word I said."

"You said so few. If it had come to trial, I'd have needed much more than you were prepared to give me. What happens if the police take it into their heads to arrest you all over again?"

"Is that why you followed me up here?"

"No."

"Then why are you here?"

He looked deep into her magnificent eyes, noting the fear that lingered in their depths. She reminded him of a wild animal, tempted to come closer and retreat at one and the same time. What had happened to her, he wondered, that she should be so suspicious of everyone? She was as pale as a ghost. She really was afraid.

"Do you mind my being here?" he asked her.

She shrugged. "Can they really arrest me all over again?"

"I suspect they only let you go because they hoped you'd make a mistake. They won't give up until they've nailed someone for Jon Ross's death. Don't worry, *hinny*, the last thing they expected you to do was to run for cover up here." He used the north-country endearment deliberately, wondering as he did so whether it had been the origin of the now more familiar American "honey."

Her body sagged. "I wanted to go straight back onto the stage, only everyone said I had to give the public time to forget all the scandal. Even my agent advised me to go away on a long holiday." She sighed heavily. "By the time they forget that, they'll have forgotten *me*, too. There are loads of talented actresses just waiting for a chance to take over. However, it didn't seem as though I had any choice."

"I'm glad you didn't go back," he said.

"Are you? Look, why are you here? It can't matter to you whether I'm innocent or guilty. What does a barrister care? I'd have thought you would have forgotten all about me long ago."

He smiled lazily. "No chance of that. What is that scent you use? The very first time I saw you, you reminded me of my little niece when she's just been tubbed and smells of soap and water and young, clean skin."

She laughed. So he bathed his little niece, did he? Somehow that made him seem a much nicer and more approachable human being. She felt suddenly at ease with him.

"I use a geranium-scented soap, or sometimes geranium-carnation." Her eyes danced with laughter. "How about you?"

He used a pine-smelling after-shave, that much she knew. It wasn't something she wanted to know. She turned her back on him, her laughter forgotten. She really didn't know why they were talking to each other at all!

She leaped to her feet. "I must be going! Nice to have seen you—"

"Going? Going where? Home to your family?"

She shook her head. "I have no family." She bit her lip. She hadn't meant to tell him that. "Mr. Wakefield, how did you know where to find me?"

"Would you believe it was sheer chance?"

He could see that she didn't. Yet it was true, as far as it went. He had stopped off, wanting to look at the wall, before going on and trying to find her at home. And yet that wasn't quite true. He had been looking around every step he had taken after he had parked the car, hoping to find her there. He hadn't even been particularly surprised when he finally saw her, resting her back against the wall, although he couldn't explain why. A romantic side of him that he'd never noticed before believed it to be fate. No way was he going to reveal to her how he had taken her address from her agent's files. He didn't think she would lightly forgive Judith for that, and her agent seemed to be the only friend she had.

"Oh well." She dismissed the whole subject, holding out her hand to him. "I hope you enjoy the rest of your holiday—somewhere else, perhaps?" Her irritation at having been discovered here, a place she had always thought of as being safe, burned anew. She turned abruptly and began to walk away from him.

"I'll walk you to your car," Aidan offered.

"Don't you want to walk the wall?" she answered through clenched teeth. "While you're here, you ought to visit Housesteads and the National Trust Centre. You'd find it very interesting—"

"I'd rather visit with you."

The simplicity of the statement brought Ruth up so sharply that she stumbled and would have fallen if he hadn't put out a hand to support her. Her flesh burned beneath his touch. She was making too much of this, she told herself. She was making too much of everything that had passed between them!

"That's because you know nothing whatever about me," she told him almost fiercely, as if she was trying to convince herself as well as him. "You wouldn't like me if you did get to know me. I'm everything the press said I am: ambitious, greedy, interested only in my career. I don't have a private life and I don't want one. Besides, you'd always remember me the way I was when we first met—in prison— and that's hardly an auspicious beginning, is it? Sometimes I think I still smell of the place."

"I can assure you you don't! Nor do I want to forget anything about you, but if you insist on having a romantic setting to our getting to know each other, what's wrong with this one?"

If he didn't know, how could she explain it to him? She had done with romance—except on the stage—and she'd do well to remember how painful disillusionment with other people's good intentions could be.

"I really must be going," she said. "I'll miss the tide if I don't leave now."

By his calculations, she had several hours before the tide would cover the narrow causeway to her home on Lindisfarne—the Holy Isle of the Dark Ages, when Northumbria had been a kingdom unto itself, neither England nor Scotland.

"We'll meet again," he was saying. Ruth supposed it was a question, still believing she had some choice in the matter.

"I hope not!" she said with a smile. "It'll mean I've been re-arrested if we do! Have a lovely end to your holiday, Mr. Wakefield."

"Aidan. I had hoped we might meet—"

No! She didn't need a man like him in her life! She didn't need anyone! She twisted her lips into a bitter smile. "You don't know what you're talking about," she told him. "I'm no good—"

"I want to see you again," he said simply.

"Why?" She cleared her throat uneasily. "Our meetings haven't been particularly auspicious so far, have they? If I were you, I wouldn't press my luck."

He was smiling and, damn him, he was getting to her. Now that she came to think of it, he did look the tiniest bit like a knight in shining armour. There was something about the features of his face, especially his firm mouth, that made her think it would be rather nice to be swept off her feet by him, which was ridiculous. She had long ago disposed of such romantic notions along with all the other rubbish of her youth. She wasn't in the market to be swept up by anyone.

"Come and have a cup of coffee before you go," he suggested. "That won't commit you to anything. I didn't have any lunch, did you?"

Ruth had meant to pack some lunch for herself, but in the end she hadn't, afraid that the tide would come in before she could get away. She had wanted to visit Hadrian's Wall again out of loneliness, a feeling she wouldn't normally admit to under any circumstances, but which was ever-present, gnawing away at any contentment she achieved and bringing her further worries about her future. Sometimes she would worry about her personal life, and sometimes about her work. It was her work bothering her right now, she insisted to herself sternly. Suppose she never got any work again?

"The National Trust sells refreshments," she heard herself saying. "We could go there if you like."

He didn't give her any chance to change her mind. Hands in his pockets, he walked easily beside her, as if he covered miles every day, instead of doing nothing more strenuous than pacing up and down a courtroom. Out of devilment, she increased the pace. Every actor has to keep fit and, despite her time on remand in prison, Ruth knew herself to be as fit as a fiddle. But so was he. He wasn't even breathing heavily when they arrived at the National Trust Centre near Housesteads Fort.

Ruth sat down at one of the picnic tables while he joined a party of pensioners on holiday in the queue to get a couple of polystyrene cups of black coffee and two packages of sandwiches. He put sugar in his own coffee, making a face as he lifted the cup to his lips.

Ruth laughed. "I can see that you don't do this often! Missing your usual haunts—proper napkins and knives and forks, and all that?"

"Aren't you?" he muttered.

She thought about it. "My standards aren't very high to begin with. They were undermined long ago by the kind of places we are given to rehearse in—some of the places we are forced to stay in when we're on tour, too!" Feeling more at ease, Ruth went on to tell him of one seaside town she had worked, where her breakfasts had been set out in advance on the mantelpiece, one individual packet of cornflakes, and one egg complete with eggcup for each day of the week ahead.

They were laughing when she finished, more companionably than they ever had before. He was a good listener and she found herself recounting how, in one well-known theatre, she had felt obliged to get down on her hands and knees and scrub the stage before she could bring herself to fall down dead on its creaking boards. "The theatre isn't all glamour and applause. Sometimes I wonder why I ever chose it as a way of life! Why did you become a lawyer?"

"Family tradition. We've been lawyers for generations. Even so, it's a hard grind getting known. I couldn't have managed without my family's backing. As it was, it was ages before I began to make any proper money. It helps if you get into good chambers—and my family connections helped me there. Then, if the clerk likes you, he can push a lot of decent briefs your way and, after a while, people begin to ask for you by name."

"By people, you mean solicitors like that wimp who was assigned to me?"

"Right. Where did you find him?"

"I didn't. Friends found him for me, said he was an admirer and would do anything for me, meaning that he wouldn't charge very much. How wrong they were! He was a theatrical hanger-on of some kind, though. At least he had met Jonathan Ross at one time, and knew his wife Sylvia."

"What kind of marriage did the Rosses have?"

She shrugged. "Theatrical marriages aren't noted for their success rate," she said.

"They'd been married for some time?"

"Oh yes, about ten years, I believe. I suppose that's as near a success as one can hope to achieve under the circumstances. I never knew either of them, you know. I'm not even sure if I really wanted to work for him. Judith thought it a good idea and she's usually right about anything to do with my career. Judith is my agent," she explained quickly, not that he had shown even by so much as a flicker that he hadn't known what she was talking about. Did he *know* Judith? It was possible. She wondered just how much he did know about Ruth Gaynor—her career, her agent, perhaps even a little about her childhood? But no, no one knew anything about that. She shivered. It wasn't something she wanted anyone to know about.

Ruth cast the man a sidelong glance and was relieved to find he wasn't even looking at her. He was making conversation, nothing more than that. She was far too sensitive for her own good! Yet she had reason to be, hadn't she? She remembered again how the police had gone on and on about what she had been doing at the Marlborough Arms that day. How much did she drink? How far she was prepared to go in order to get a good, juicy part? And here she was at thirty and still a virgin and practically unkissed—though no one would believe that.

Ruth didn't have the time to walk the quarter-mile to the fort, but determined now to end this meeting once and for all, she firmly recommended it to Aidan. She walked with him as far as the gate that led to the steep path across the valley to the fort.

"Watch out for the Galloway cattle on the way," Ruth teased him, annoyed with herself because it was suddenly very hard to see him go.

"Those shaggy creatures with fringes that get in their eyes?"

Her eyes travelled the route he was about to take. "Actually, there seem to be more sheep than cattle," she said.

"Mostly Swaledale," he confirmed, surprising her all over again.

The smooth image of the London barrister didn't go very deep, she thought, though it had deceived her for some time. What did he know about sheep and cattle, she wondered, that he could recognise one of the local breeds so easily? Ruth opened her eyes wide. "You'd know all about that, of course!" she exclaimed sarcastically.

"A bit. When I get nearer to retirement, I shall return to my childhood haunts, buy a small farm and have a rest from the criminal fraternity. Wouldn't you like to live on a farm?"

Ruth had thought so once. Years ago, when she had first been orphaned and was living with the woman she had thought of as her aunt, she had been friendly with a farmer and his wife. It had been her ambition to grow up fast and have a farm of her own. For a time she had kept in touch with the Jenkinses, after she had left her aunt's care. She had not seen them very often, but often enough to be saddened by her own ambitions, which would take her away from the familiar routines she had once wanted. The Jenkinses had not understood her obsession with the stage, and she had been quite unable to explain it to them. She wondered if they still lived in the same place and whether they would receive her if she were to visit them. It would be fun to see them again.

"I'll stick with what I know. The theatre is my first and only love." She knew it was a lie as she said it. Over the past week her love for the north country had been reborn. It was better if he didn't suspect they had anything in common—she knew nothing would come of it.

Aidan wondered what had caused the sudden shadow in her eyes. He would have liked to ask her what had taken her onto the stage in the first place, but he was afraid of her retreating back into herself again. She did that far too often as it was. He doubted she was a natural as an actress, however. It was an insecure profession at best and she seemed to have started from nothing, with no family in the business. He wondered how many times she had gone to bed hungry and questioned her desire to be an actress.

"Ruth, what are you going to do with yourself now?"

"I'll get work soon. Judith will see to that. She's one of the best agents around."

Aidan felt as though she were physically pushing him away. Very well, Miss Gaynor, he thought, he would let her get away now, but it would only be a temporary escape. He would follow her to her house on Lindisfarne and—one never knew—she might be sufficiently surprised to be glad to see him. At least she didn't dislike him.

He held out his hands to her. "I believe you didn't have anything to do with the murder," he said. "But something happened to you to make you suspicious of anyone who comes anywhere near you. I'm warning you, Ruth, my dear, I mean to stick around until I find out what it is."

She looked at him in blank amazement. She had the most expressive face. He watched her reaction change from indignation to a fearful hope and, finally, to complete rejection of him and his intentions.

"No! I don't need you. I don't need anyone!"

"We all need someone," Aidan gently insisted.

Not she! Ruth thought. It would take her five minutes to reach her car, she calculated. If she ran all the way she might do it in less. Would he follow her? "What do you want from me?" she said despairingly.

"I want to kiss you," he said, his voice husky. "I've wanted to kiss you from the first moment I saw you."

"Well, I *don't* want to kiss you!"

"I know, but only because you're afraid you might like it."

Ruth rubbed her tongue over dry lips, considering what he said seriously. "That's got nothing to do with it. Good heavens, why should I be afraid of that?"

"You'll miss the tide," Aidan reminded her, taking her hand. "You'd better run away while you still can. I'm going to be one step behind you all the way."

"You don't know where I live," she said, mesmerized by his gentle voice.

"Don't I?" he asked.

His question broke the spell. She pulled her hand away from his, ashamed because she had liked the contact more than she thought she should. "You won't be able to find me. Nobody has my address! It's my own private place and I don't invite anyone to come there. I don't want you. And I don't need you! If you know what's good for you, you'll stay as far away from me as you possibly can!"

Aidan watched her walk away, admiring her smooth grace and the straightness of her back. She was a proud woman, and he liked that about her. An orphan she might be, lonely she certainly was, and as stubborn as a mule, but she was also an incredibly attractive and desirable woman, a sleeping princess waiting for Prince Charming to come along. It wasn't a role in which he would normally have cast himself, but he suspected Miss Ruth Gaynor was well worth its disadvantages. He waved his hand to her, smiling. "Look out, my *hinny*," he said aloud, "you can run as fast and as far as you want, I'll still be right behind you. I'll be there before you know it and we'll start by having dinner together."

Chapter Two

Lindisfarne, Ruth's home had a name to conjure with, a name to evoke heroes, saints of old, and events long past. Add to it its other title, Holy Island, she thought, driving toward the causeway, and the very air breathed of history. Those must have been the days, when the old Celtic Church had decided to make the change to the Roman calendar, so that all Christians could celebrate the major feasts together, on the same day of the year. It was in those days that St. Aidan had first come to Northumberland from that other Holy Island, Iona in Scotland, not speaking a word of English and having to rely on the sainted King Oswald to walk from one village to another by his side, translating his every word. The people had flocked to hear his words. By the time of his death, the whole kingdom was ripe to fall into the hands of his much loved successor, St. Cuthbert. Ruth smiled to think that the locals still talked about him as if they had met him face-to-face only the day before.

Lindisfarne was the only place in the world that she could ever consider home. Orphaned at an early age, Ruth barely remembered Melissa Moir, the woman who had first taken her in when her parents had died. Ruth had been happy in Lindisfarne, but there had been confusion and a sense of loss when she was taken away from the woman, for reasons that had never been disclosed to her. As Ruth grew older she understood that Melissa Moir had been a single woman of indeterminate age and seemed more interested in her painting than in living to the kind of timetable most people thought best for a young child. Consequently, it had come as an enormous surprise to Ruth when she learned that the old lady had died and left Ruth all of her possessions, including the house on Lindisfarne. Ruth had wondered if they weren't related after all, but nobody she asked knew anything much about Miss Moir. Ruth came to think of Miss Moir as an orphan like herself, who had had no relations to whom she could leave her possessions. Perhaps Miss Moir had thought of Ruth as someone as much on her own as she had always been. No relatives had come forward to claim any part of the woman's estate and, since Ruth had been coming to the house in Lindisfarne, no one had ever questioned her right to be there.

I couldn't give you a refuge in my lifetime, Miss Moir had written in a letter the solicitor had sent her, *but I am giving you one now. Every person should be able to be independent of others, no matter what her state in life. Don't be tempted to part with the only inheritance you will probably ever receive in this life, no matter what the price.*

Ruth had taken the advice to heart. The joys of owning property were very real to someone who had never had anything permanent. Ruth had spent her childhood in one foster home after another. In her adult life she'd lived in a variety of theatrical digs, all of which had had a temporary

air and none of which had ever been home to her. But, for
the three years following Miss Moir's death, Lindisfarne was
where she could escape to when she needed to be alone, to
rest after the lengthy run of a play, or to think herself into a
new part. There she could pretend to herself that she wasn't
desperate for the next part to keep body and soul together.
Lindisfarne was the only thing in Ruth's life that had never
failed her.

It wasn't really an island. At low tide one could drive over
the causeway from the mainland. At high tide, though,
twice each day, Lindisfarne retreated into itself. The visi-
tors were gone and it caught its breath and regained its re-
pose before the next invasion of tourists arrived, seeking the
peculiar elusive charm that made it famous throughout
Britain.

Ruth started out over the stone causeway and breathed a
sigh of relief. She was only just in time to catch the tide. A
few minutes later and the water would have been lapping at
the feet of the white-painted refuge designed for those who
got caught halfway across. It had been a longer drive from
Hadrian's Wall than she had remembered and she was tired;
tired of the road, and tired of her own thoughts, which quite
unaccountably dwelled on Aidan Wakefield and what had
brought him to the north of England.

It was unlikely, she thought, that he would find his way
to her house in Lindisfarne. Oh, he might come as a tourist
amongst a thousand others, but she kept well out of the way
of the popular haunts at those times of the day. Ruth had
plenty to do in her own house. And yet, she almost wished
he would find her. How was it possible that she should feel
this sudden need for company—she, who had never allowed herself to feel the least bit lonely in the past?

She parked her car in the small space and reached over
into the back seat for the provisions and other oddments she

had bought earlier that day. If there were one snag with her house, Ruth thought, it was that it always seemed a bit damp to her. It was probably because she was able to use it so seldom, shutting it up for weeks at a time whenever she was working down South. Whenever she was staying at the house, no matter what the time of year, she kept fires going in all the grates. Luckily, there were almost as many fireplaces as there were rooms. Tonight, with a damp mist blowing in from the sea, the expected epilogue to a sunny day, Ruth was looking forward to building a nice peat fire. It would bring a flame of cheer to the chimney—and to her heart.

As Ruth felt in her pocket for her front door key a prickling sensation on the back of her neck warned her she was being watched. It took a positive act of will to remind herself how unlikely it was that anyone was going to mug her or steal from her in the secluded safety of Lindisfarne.

"What kept you?" she heard Aidan Wakefield ask, and Ruth turned around. The dreadful thing was that she couldn't have been more pleased to see anyone. Her whole being wanted to shout out a welcome to him. Worse, when he smiled in quite that way, she could feel the ice in which she had long ago enclosed her emotions begin to crack, bringing a delicious, hitherto never experienced excitement.

"Did you expect to lose me so easily?" he mocked.

"Who gave you my address?" She knew she sounded both prim and disapproving. What a blessing it was that she could still act her way out of what looked to be an increasingly awkward situation.

His expression told her he wasn't fooled as he took her key out of her hand and opened the door for her. Aidan would be a difficult man to deceive, she thought, once he had made up his mind to get down to the truth. How much did that matter to her? Not very much, she decided, because not even she knew the truth about herself.

"You realize," she said, "that you can't get back to the mainland for hours. The tide was coming in fast when I came over the causeway."

"I thought I might stay a day or two," he said, innocence personified.

"Oh, you did, did you? Well, you needn't think you're staying with me!" They might as well get that straight from the start. It wasn't a particularly spacious cottage for one person. Besides, she simply wasn't that kind of woman. "You may come in for a cup of tea, if you want to," she added grudgingly.

"Ah, the national panacea," he murmured with approval. "Do you want this bag of peat taken inside?"

"Please."

He followed her inside, taking a good look round her small, old-fashioned home, hugging the brown paper bag of peat to him. "This is nice!" he approved. "I can see why you think a fire's in order, however. Shall I get started on one in the sitting room while you put the kettle on?"

She was amused at the easy way he organized things to suit him, even in her house. "If you think you can. There's quite an art in lighting fires in these old grates."

She needn't have worried. Aidan was as good with fires as he was at eliciting information from his clients. With Ruth, the hearth was apt to sulk until she had succeeded in warming it up, but he, by holding an old newspaper in front to cause a draught, had his kindling blazing away in a matter of seconds.

When Aidan was satisfied that the logs had caught, he stood up and examined the few watercolours that were hanging on the walls.

"Your choice?" he asked her.

"Miss Moir's. I think she was quite an artist. They say on the island that she made some kind of a living out of her painting. I don't think she was anyone famous, however, though recently I've had a lot of telephone calls asking if I have any Melissa Moirs to sell. I don't want to part with them, though. They came with the house, and here they'll stay."

"Is that what you told your callers?"

"Every time," she told him cheerfully. "It's not as if the paintings are really valuable. Somebody would have come after them long ago if that had been the case."

He looked at her with interest. "You told me you had no family," he reminded her.

"I haven't."

"What about this aunt?"

Ruth stared at him, resenting the inquisition, especially since she hadn't any answers. She knew only the barest of details about Miss Moir. "She wasn't actually related to me. I lived with her for a while, that's all. She died three years ago. The lawyers told me she didn't have anyone else, which was why she left me this house in her will. Before then, I had almost forgotten about her. Children don't remember very much about their earliest years, you know. Satisfied?"

"Didn't you ever go back to see her?"

"No."

Ruth made the tea, stirring it thoughtfully with a spoon while she considered the best way of dealing with Aidan and his questions. It would have been easier if she was less aware of him, or if she knew what he was doing here, making himself at home in her cottage. What did he want from her? Only a kiss? That she most certainly did not believe; nor could she possibly allow it. Ruth felt a quiver of fear at the thought. It was far safer for her to send him away as quickly as she could. She was better off alone—as she always had been.

Ruth poured out two cups, placing the milk and sugar where Aidan could reach them and taking her own cup to one of the easy chairs on either side of the fireplace. "All I'm saying is," she went on defensively, "that if you've never had a family, you don't feel the need for one. I was taken away from Miss Moir when I was six years old and was fostered out with various other families until I was sixteen and considered old enough to look after myself."

"Whereupon you went down to London to make a career for yourself? Didn't you ever want to know about this 'aunt,' to find out if you were really related to her or not?"

She shook her head. "I was a different person by that time. Besides, I could hardly remember her at all. That's why I was so astonished when she left me this house and everything in it. That was three years ago. I came up here from time to time after that, but I've been too busy to do more than look in for the occasional weekend. I was even thinking of selling it and had an agent come and look it over. When it came to it, though, I couldn't do it. The only thing she had asked of me was to hang on to the house. I'm glad I did now. At least I have a roof over my head."

His expression baffled her. He was watching her as carefully as he had in prison, but not by a flicker of an eyelid did he betray what he was thinking. Fleetingly, she was beguiled by the pensive beauty of his face as he glanced towards the fire and stooped to replenish the peat to feed the flames. For the first time, she consciously thought of him as a man with needs and feelings of his own, rather than as an undefined threat that had to be warded off at all costs for no better reason than because she didn't trust anyone.

He had borne with her efforts to be rid of him pretty well, all things considered. She remembered their first meeting as if it had been yesterday. Aidan had whirled into the interview room as if he owned the whole prison. Ruth had been stunned by the impact he made on her. For a long time there she had forgotten to feel sorry for herself and had felt a spark of her usual liveliness come back to life within her.

Aidan's approach had been refreshingly different, appealing to her pride not to be beaten by the system, no matter how she felt about it. Looking back, she wondered how he had known that only that challenge would work with her just then. She had been fighting the system ever since she could remember, but he couldn't have known that.

It was that ability he had of being able to put himself in her place that made her doubly cautious of accepting anything from him now. Why was he here at all?

"Where are you planning on spending the night?" Ruth said abruptly. She didn't want to think of him sleeping in his car and, if he was stranded, they had to start looking for a place for him to stay. She eyed him thoughtfully. If he thought she was going to be a soft touch because she was grateful to him, the sooner she disabused his mind of any such idea the better! She wasn't in the market for any man. She *preferred* being on her own. It was much more comfortable and far less trouble in the long run.

Ruth sighed, not wanting to hurt his feelings. Her gaze softened as she looked at him. He wasn't conventionally handsome, not compared to some of the men she was accustomed to, but he was hard and lean and he had an odd, dark beauty that gave her a jolt every time she set eyes on him. Earlier that day, she had even wondered what it would be like to be kissed by him. Now her imagination was suddenly aflame with as many seductive images of him as there were flames to the fire. Perhaps she was finally going out of her mind. Men simply didn't have this effect on her!

Aidan suppressed a laugh, seeing embarrassment and interest mingled in Ruth's expression. "I found myself a room with a neighbour of yours before I drove up here, so you needn't worry that I'm intending to take advantage of you in any way. If you were to offer me dinner, though, I wouldn't say no. I didn't see many restaurants on my drive through the village."

She sniffed. "As long as that's as far as it goes." Ruth's tone of voice gave nothing away about the leap her heart took at the thought of having him to herself for a little longer. It would be the first time she had ever entertained anyone, man or woman, in her own home. Not even Judith, her friend as well as her agent, had troubled to come this far north to visit her.

"You'll always be quite safe with me," Aidan broke into her thoughts, his voice like thick honey. "I shan't ever hurt you."

That was easy enough to say! Ruth thought. Aidan Wakefield was too clever by half when it came to getting his own way, taking charge as if he had every right to do so, just as he had when he had visited her in prison. What did he want from her?

Ruth smiled grimly at the confident hands he was holding out to her, but she found herself extending her own just the same, enjoying the contact of his palms against hers.

"Nothing will happen between us that you don't want to happen," he sought to reassure her. "You have my word on it. If we don't get to know each other, though, how are we ever going to find out what really happened to you that day? I can't help you if I don't know."

"I'd much rather forget all about it!"

His eyes held hers, burning through her defences. "Can you?"

She sighed. "No, I'll never forget." Her lips trembled. "I don't think I could go through that experience again, Aidan." It was the first time she had called him by his given name, but only he noticed. "I couldn't stand to go back to prison."

"Then we'll have to make sure that you never do. Cheer up, love, there has to be a logical explanation. All we have to do is find it." He touched her cheek and ran his fingers along the line of her jaw, going from there to the thin scar that still showed clearly on her arm. "There you go. Aren't you glad I came now?"

"Yes, I am," Ruth admitted.

"So am I."

The words were soft and intimate, sending shivers of pleasure up and down her spine. What an actor he would have made with a voice like that! She considered him thoughtfully. In a way, a barrister had to be something of an actor, she supposed. He had to have the same timing, the same ability to command attention and, very often, she had no doubt, the same liking for applause when a job was well done. Suddenly she felt she understood Mr. Aidan Wakefield and liked him very much, perhaps too much for her own good. It was a long time since she had allowed herself the luxury of really liking anyone. She had been far too afraid of being hurt. How was it that this particular man had undermined her defences so that she was able to admit out loud that she was glad to have him in her house—and might even like to have him come closer still?

Ruth took a hasty sip of tea and smiled up at him lazily. "I might easily not have been here at all," she told him. "I might have been working."

"I'd have found you in the end," Aidan said, returning the smile.

"The determined type?" She already knew the answer to that. Ruth could see it in the strength of his face and the way his eyes seemed able to read her most intimate thoughts. The only thing she couldn't understand was why he should bother with her. Nobody else ever had.

"In this case," he replied.

Her eyes dropped. "Actually there was very little chance I'd be working," she confessed. "I've always been told that in our profession any publicity is better than none, but it didn't work out quite like that for me. Judith, my agent, said people were a bit cagey at the moment. She meant they were afraid I might get my knife into *them*—" She broke off, her lips twisted in pain. "Sorry, that was a bad slip, wasn't it?"

"I've heard worse." His face creased with concern for her.

She made a small shrug of apology. "Yes, well, I'm a bit worried as to when it'll stop." She frowned. "I don't know why I should be telling you all this. You can't possibly be interested. The thing is that I need to get work—and quickly. When I first began on the stage I was hardly ever working at all—*resting*, we call it. The temporary jobs I got by on were far from being restful, though, let me tell you! But at least one could *get* jobs in those days. I doubt one could get temporary waitressing, filling shelves in supermarkets or even cleaning these days!"

"There's always the dole," he pointed out.

She made a face at him. "The state paid for my childhood. I ought to be standing on my own two feet by now, don't you think?"

Aidan's reaction was not as she'd expected. He didn't tell her she was being silly, as Judith had done. He simply stared at her, his coal-black eyes full of worry.

"I don't like to think of you living from hand to mouth," he said.

"What actress doesn't live that way?" She tried to dismiss her own fears. "Judith will come up with something sooner or later. Judith always does, even if it's only a voice-over on an advertisement."

"Do you do much of that sort of thing?"

She nodded. "It's very well paying. I still get royalties from an advertisement I did nearly three years ago." She forced a laugh. "You can thank that advertisement for your dinner tonight!"

Ruth watched as Aidan sipped his tea, fascinated by the movement of his mouth. This was getting to be ridiculous, she chastised herself. First, she had bleated out her troubles to him—she, who never told anyone anything she could help about herself—and now she couldn't keep her eyes off him, hungry to observe every movement he made.

Unfortunately, Aidan chose that moment to look up and catch her staring at him. In his place, she would have been disconcerted, but his only reaction was to laugh out loud. His expression contained such complete masculine satisfaction at her interest that she could feel her cheeks begin to glow with embarrassment.

She averted her gaze, pulling her skirt down over her knees. Finally, she stood up and disappeared into the kitchen before he could say anything else to put her on edge.

"I'm afraid it's chicken or chicken," she called out to Aidan. Suddenly, he put a hand on her shoulder and the shock of it travelled right down to her toes. He was so close behind her that she gasped. Slowly, he pulled her back against the hard wall of his chest, his arms enclosing her completely. Ruth shut her eyes, reminding herself of all the reasons for not allowing him to get too close to her. It didn't make the slightest difference; her heart was still hammering against her ribs, and there was a burgeoning glow to her whole body. If this went on, she would be his for the taking, and that she simply couldn't allow.

"I like chicken," Aidan said.

He turned her round to face him and she studied the top button of his shirt and the tanned, smooth skin of his neck, her thoughts in a whirl. If she were to look any higher she would drown in those dark eyes of his and then she'd be lost forever.

Slowly, gently, he kissed her. She felt the tip of his tongue against her lips and swallowed convulsively. His tongue slipped past her lips and explored her mouth, tangling lazily with her own tongue. It was the most sensual kiss she had ever received—and it scared her to death. She felt like a puppet in his hands, unable to control her reactions, or to make a single movement.

"I like the taste of you," he whispered with a note of satisfaction.

She rallied her defences with determination. "You wouldn't if you knew me better."

Aidan smiled straight into those fantastic eyes of hers, holding her head between his two open hands. He felt her quiver and wondered at how easy it was to throw her off balance. Nobody looking at her now would believe she was thirty years old and had earned her living for half that time on the stage. Where had all the men been in her life?

She rescued her hands from where they had been placed against his chest, only to rub them against his roughened beard. He probably had to shave twice a day...

"How about a chicken curry?" she asked weakly.

He let her go with a flattering reluctance, dropping a light kiss on the end of her nose. "Good idea! If you'll allow me into your kitchen, I'll cook you a curry you'll remember all the days of your life! I'm a dab hand at curry and rice. It's one of the dishes I do best."

She felt like laughing, though she didn't know why. "You cook, too?"

"I'd starve if I didn't," he answered cheerfully.

Her curiosity was piqued. "Don't your girlfriends cook for you?"

"From time to time. There are usually strings attached to that kind of arrangement, I find. I prefer to feed my women, rather than have them feed me."

She found she didn't like to think of the army of women he must have fed in his time. "Isn't that a bit arrogant?" she challenged.

"Perhaps. Whom do you cook for, Ruth?"

"Myself," she admitted.

"Don't you ever feed your boyfriends?"

"No. Nothing is for nothing is my motto in life! I neither issue nor accept invitations from most of the people I know."

"That's because you've never met the one who'd turn all those ideas of yours on their head. I'd do quite a lot for you, my prickly beauty, without any payment at all, if you wanted me to."

"You're not my type," she insisted.

He busied himself getting the chicken out of the refrigerator. He dumped it in the middle of the table, taking the opportunity to point an accusing finger at her. "Well, it might as well be me as anyone else. I have many good points, I'll have you know, and I've no intention of allowing you to overlook any of them. As soon as you've got used to having me about, and have got to know me better—"

"I don't want to know you any better!"

"You forget I'm specially trained to distinguish lies from the truth when I hear them. That was a great, black lie." He smiled intimately at her. "Your trouble is that you've never given yourself an opportunity to find out what you want in a man. Well, that's all right with me. We all have to begin with someone, and it will shortly occur to you that you may as well begin with an up-and-coming barrister of good prospects, without any entanglements to get in the way. Don't you find that a fascinating prospect?"

"It sounds like a pipe dream to me," she said before she realized how he would interpret her words. His mocking glance brought a rush of colour to her cheeks.

"My point exactly. Feel free to dream about me all you wish. I'd say we've made a most satisfactory beginning, wouldn't you?"

She chewed on her lower lip. "A beginning to what?"

"A beginning to whatever you want it to be."

Her eyes met his, soft and scared. "I don't want—" She began again. "It's safer never to begin anything. You'll be going back to London soon and you'll forget all about me—"

"Rubbish!" he cut her off, biting out the word with such force that she just stood there, staring at him, shocked by the strength of her feelings. He went on more gently, "We both know we've been wanting to kiss since the first moment we set eyes on each other. Why pretend about it?"

"I didn't know that!" she wailed, uncomfortably aware that her statement was nearer to being a lie than the truth.

He grinned at her. "Well, you know now." His expression softened at the fevered glitter in her eyes. "It's nothing to get upset about, *hinny*. When I kiss you again later on, you'll find it doesn't hurt at all."

"I'd much rather you did no such thing. If you knew all about me—"

"Tell me," he invited her.

"I don't even know who I am, not really," she began. "All I know about myself is my name—"

"You know Miss Moir took care of you as a child. She must have had a connection to your family."

"I suppose so. But don't you think it odd she should have left her house to me? Didn't she have any real family? Was there no one else?"

"Did anyone come to her funeral?"

"I don't know. I didn't go myself. She was dead and buried before the solicitor got in touch with me and told me about the house. He said there had been some difficulty over getting the will proved, but he never told me the details. I suppose he thought it was none of my business."

"Perhaps you didn't ask?"

She hung her head. "Perhaps I didn't. It took me a while to get used to the idea that anyone would want to leave me anything. Oh dear, that sounds a bit mawkish, doesn't it? But I'm used to having no one of my own—and then this! I wouldn't allow myself to believe it for ages, just in case it wasn't really true. Silly, isn't it?" She steadied herself, ashamed she had already revealed so much to him, a stranger, no matter how attractive he was to her. She would be telling him next that, despite her thirty years, she had always been too afraid to get emotionally involved with a man, that she wasn't learned in the ways of love, as he seemed to be. Ruth felt a dull regret that she had never learned to relate to others as most people did.

She watched Aidan start making their curry, enjoying his neat, economical movements. He showed no signs of being shocked by what she had said. Ruth felt comforted by the fact. She wouldn't have told anyone else half of what she had already told him. He had such a soothing manner about him as he casually threw ingredients together that she wouldn't have dreamed of putting in a curry. Her own method was completely different from his spontaneity. She always measured out each ingredient exactly, as if she were conducting a scientific experiment. Ruth suspected Aidan probably ended up with better results than she did.

"May I cook the rice?" she asked, humbled by his easy mastery of the kitchen.

"Good idea! We may as well get used to cooking together."

She ignored his words. "You may not like the way I cook rice," she pointed out.

"I'll like it." His dark eyes caressed her. "I like everything about you. Haven't you realized that yet?"

She doubted he meant a word of what he was saying, but it was nice to pretend for a while that he did. There was something companionable about sharing the kitchen, getting in each other's way. They didn't talk much, but they both got hungrier and hungrier as the chicken simmered with the onions and spices, adding an enticing aroma to the steamy air.

"Hot, or very hot?" he asked her.

She peered into the pot. "Very hot," she said eagerly.

"Good," he said, "that's how I like it, too."

Chapter Three

Over dinner, Ruth began to laugh as Aidan told her story after story about his experiences with the law. She had never thought she could laugh like that. Her surprise made her stop and stare at Aidan as though she had never seen him before.

"I haven't laughed like that for simply ages," she exclaimed.

"I'm glad I amuse you," he rejoined, his dark eyes glimmering with an intimacy that made her lower hers in an old-fashioned gesture that he thought was so much a part of her.

"Oh, you do," she said.

It was his turn to laugh. "It's much better than making you cry."

Ruth was immediately concerned that she might have hurt his feelings by being unfriendly. She wondered whether she should confess to him how afraid she had been of everybody recently. She had thought at first her sense of danger had all been in her imagination, and yet—and yet—

She recalled Melissa Moir's solicitor, who had first told her about her inheritance. Miss Moir had been an odd woman, he had told her—almost a recluse. The elderly solicitor had been about to retire the following week, and clearing up the details of Miss Moir's will had been the last bit of legal work he had done.

Ruth had asked him if Miss Moir hadn't had any family of her own. The old man had become quite cross at the question, she remembered, adjusting his spectacles on his nose with impatient fingers.

"That has nothing to do with you, young lady," he had said. "She wanted you to have the Lindisfarne cottage and its contents, and that's all you need to know."

Ruth had liked the old man. It hadn't concerned her that when she had timidly suggested he might advertise Miss Moir's death, he had told her to mind her own business. He had done it quite kindly, his eyes twinkling at her beneath bushy brows.

"She didn't want any publicity, my dear. She had little to do with people in life, why should anyone be interested in her death?"

A small, damp cottage on Lindisfarne probably wouldn't have meant much to anyone, one way or the other, Ruth had reasoned. If her inheritance had been a gold-plated mansion, with a bank balance to go with it, Ruth might have pressed him further. As it was, she had rejoiced in her own good fortune and had gone blithely on her way.

But once she had moved into the cottage there had been those peculiar telephone calls. And then there was the time she thought someone had tried to break in. She had begun to wonder if Miss Moir's unknown relatives hadn't resented the woman's choice of heir. If they *had* wanted to contest the will there would have been nothing to stop them from doing it in an open way. But Ruth's fears had grown, especially when she was alone in the cottage with only shadows and her imagination for company. How had Melissa Moir kept body and soul together without any means of support? The Lindisfarne villagers had told her with surprise that Miss Moir had lived on income from the sales of her paintings, and Ruth had pictured an elderly, wind-swept woman setting up her latest works outside her own front door and selling the paintings to the tourists for only a few pounds each. The woman certainly hadn't had any money to spend on the house. Until Ruth had painted it up a bit, it looked as if no one had touched it for years and years.

Suddenly, Ruth wanted to share her thoughts with Aidan. "Had you ever heard of Melissa Moir before today?" she asked him. Her voice was low and compelling and she tensed as he took a minute to think about his answer.

"The name is familiar," he admitted at last. "Wasn't it to you?"

"I'd known of her since I was a baby. I just wondered if she didn't have a family after all. Her solicitor wouldn't tell me."

His expression was kindly. "I don't suppose they would mind your inheriting this place, if that's what worrying you."

"I feel uncomfortable not knowing anything about her circumstances. What if her own family was in need?"

"What did her solicitor say?"

"He told me to mind my own business."

"Well, there you are then. He didn't sound worried that anyone would try to take your cottage away from you."

"He's dead. He'd practically retired when Miss Moir died. He died soon after his retirement."

"But you never heard anything from her relatives, did you? If they'd wanted to contest the will, you'd have heard soon enough."

That was what *she* thought. Ruth smiled sleepily at him. "In a minute you're going to tell me I worry too much," she accused him. "Maybe I do, but I can't help feeling that someone is watching me. When you came upon me at the wall, I thought you might have been one of them."

"One of whom?"

She shrugged her shoulders. "I don't know. I can't explain how I feel. Don't pay any attention to me. I think this whole business has affected my mind as well as my dreams!"

Aidan leaned back in his chair, smiling. "Tell me about your dreams, Ruth Gaynor," he murmured, trying to calm her. He didn't like to see fear in her lovely eyes.

She shook her head. "They wouldn't interest you. They're all to do with the theatre. I love it. I can depend on other men's words. I envy you, Aidan, that you make up your own as you go along, and it all comes out making sense. What made you want to be a barrister?"

"I'll tell you when I know you better," he said, gently mocking her earlier reticence.

She looked at him, trying to penetrate the shadows that hid his eyes from her. "Are you going to know me better?"

He reached down and threw another log on the fire, packing it round with pieces of peat. The aromatic smoke it gave off scented the air of the room.

"I'm going to know you much better," he averred.

Ruth veiled her eyes deliberately, pretending to herself that she hadn't felt the slight quickening of her heartbeat that his words had caused. It was a feeling she had portrayed a hundred times on the stage and screen, and yet she had never really felt it in her own body before. She was shocked at how different the excitement was in reality. Suddenly, she was afraid again. If this went on, where would her independence be?

"I'm not sure I want you to know me," she said aloud. "You may not like what you find."

Aidan was silent for so long that she thought he wasn't going to answer at all. When he did speak, she felt again that thrust of excitement under her ribs. "Have you so many secrets, Ruth?" he asked her.

"Secrets?" The idea was a novel one to her. "I don't know what you mean."

"Why won't I like what I find?"

Startled, she looked at him fully then. His dark eyes seemed to swallow her up. "I don't even know who I am," she said.

"Do any of us?"

She saw that he didn't understand what she was talking about. People who had always been part of a secure family seldom did. "You have your own secrets," she told him. "I don't even know what mine are. If there are skeletons in my family's cupboard, I'll never know. That's why I can't share my secrets with you."

"Okay, so you don't know who your parents are. What's that got to do with you?"

"You *do* know who yours are. You know the sort of people they are. I don't."

"True. I happen to like my parents, but I am separate from them. I don't live their lives and they don't live mine. You've done thirty years of living on your own. That's all I want to know about."

"No, you don't," she snapped. "You want to know if I killed Jonathan! You haven't believed my story for one minute, have you? Why not? Because I don't have anyone respectable to speak up for me?"

Shocked, Aidan stared at her for a long moment. "My God, you're bitter, aren't you? Is that what we did to you by putting you in prison?"

"*You* didn't do anything to me!" she protested.

His smile was lazy and—affectionate was the only word for it. "So what is it that you do hold against me?"

"Nothing," she said softly.

"Oh yes, there's something, and I'm not going to rest until I know what it is!"

Ruth was rather shocked. She wondered why he should be sufficiently interested in her to want to know. Of course, he was right in thinking there was something she held against him, but she wasn't sure what it was. Was it his confidence in a whole area of life where she had always felt excluded and lost? Perhaps. But more than that, she didn't want to have to dredge up answers out of her subconscious. She feared she wouldn't much like the answers.

Ruth licked her lips, swallowing hard when she realized that he had read her actions as an invitation. Damn the man! He didn't miss a trick.

"I'm a very private person," she said at last. "I don't enjoy being put under a microscope for someone else's entertainment."

He leaned forward. "Is that why you think I want to know?"

She cursed her vulnerability, but she wasn't going to lie about it. "We're going round in circles," she complained. "Only you can know why you came all this way to find out something about me. I can't help it if you're disappointed, can I? I could have told you when I first saw you there was nothing to know."

"Is that why you're an actress?" he said sharply. "Because you don't know how to play yourself?"

"Maybe," Ruth snapped.

"Never mind, love," he said quietly. "I rather like the real you—what I know of her. That's why I'm here. I caught a glimpse of the woman and I wanted to get to know you better. There's nothing frightening in that, is there?"

Ruth veiled her eyes so that he couldn't read her thoughts. "I don't know," she said. She thought she sounded sullen and ungrateful and wished she could be more gracious. Then she laughed. "So that's why you came, because you liked the look of me! Poor Aidan. What a disappointment for you."

"Why?"

"Well, because!" Suddenly she looked haughty and beautifully regal. "If I didn't sleep to get parts in the theatre, why should I sleep with you?"

Aidan chuckled, throwing her off balance. "I do know that much about you. You may be a good actress, my love, but I would never believe you if you told me you'd slept with a hundred men."

Ruth's face burned crimson. She didn't know why she should resent his guessing she was still a virgin, but she did. Come to think of it, she resented everything about him. She didn't need Aidan Wakefield pushing her around; even less did she need him in her house, eating her food and making a fool of her. Ruth considered asking him to go, but something held her back. Her mind filled with the memories of the disbelief of the police when she had denied knowing Jonathan before the fateful day. None of *them* had believed her, so why should Aidan? Perhaps he was still trying to trap her into making an admission that would finally put her in her place—that is, back in prison! "I wish you hadn't come!" she said finally.

He reached out, taking her hands in his, kissing first one palm and then the other. "You'll get used to my being here, love—in time. What shall we do tomorrow?"

"Tomorrow?" She snatched her hands away from him. "*We* aren't going to do anything—are we?" Ruth said, confused by his not having taken offence.

"You can show me the island," he suggested softly.

With determination, she shook her head. "When the tides turn, you ought to go. There's nothing to do here. When all the tourists have gone it can get quite lonely. It isn't at all your cup of tea."

"You'd know about that, of course," he mocked her. "You sit there and think up some more reasons why I should go back to London and I'll do the washing up."

The man was defying her every wish. What right had he? "Indeed you won't!" She hesitated at the pleading expression on his face. "I'm not being a very good hostess, am I? You see, Lindisfarne is special to me, but you're the city type. There aren't any lights and jazzy entertainment around here. You have to go to Berwick for that, and even then you'll probably be disappointed."

"Very likely," he agreed cheerfully.

"Well then," she persevered, "you don't want to waste your holiday, do you?"

"Can't I like Lindisfarne, too?"

Aidan's sincere expression caught her off guard, but Ruth didn't deign to answer. If she was going to help him do the washing up, she might as well get on with it. She picked up their dirty plates and removed them to the kitchen.

"Turn on the television if you want to," she instructed over her shoulder. It felt like her last line of defence for, if he were to take over her kitchen again, the next thing he would take over would be her, and what would she do then?

The light in the kitchen was a single globe, hanging only by a wire that should have been designated a danger to life and limb some twenty years before. It was very badly placed, too, so that one was always standing in one's light.

For that reason, when Ruth was on her own, she always left the washing up for the morning. Then she would waste time staring out the window towards Lindisfarne Castle, the dreamy fortress that seemed to rise out of nowhere and that Melissa Moir had painted again and again. Ruth could see why.

Aidan appeared in the doorway, an open book in his hand. "What do you mean there's nothing to see on Lindisfarne? What about the castle? What about Gertrude Jekyll's garden? What about—"

At her wit's end, Ruth captured a strand of hair that had fallen onto her forehead and put it behind her ear. "Are you some kind of gardening expert?" she demanded, facing him.

"I know who Gertrude Jekyll was, if that's what you mean." He sounded amused.

Ruth remembered her own ignorance of Gertrude Jekyll, gardener extraordinaire, and how she had mistaken her portrait in the castle for one of Queen Victoria when she had first seen it.

"She often used to work with Lutyens. He was the one who restored the castle, wasn't he?" said Aidan with an innocent expression on his face.

She cast him a look of dislike. She could see his education had been worth every penny his parents had paid for it. She sniffed. "She designed the walled garden. You can see it from the castle."

"Are you going to show it to me?" he asked, excitement twinkling in his brown eyes.

Ruth sniffed again to show Aidan she knew far more about the area than he did. "I should have thought you were a member of the National Trust. The castle and garden belong to them."

He grinned at her, amused that she wanted to impress him. "Aren't you a member?"

She nodded. The National Trust was one of her passions in life. Even the story of its beginning was romantic, all mixed up as it was with the illustrator and writer, Beatrix Potter, well-loved creator of *Peter Rabbit*, and that lady's properties in the Lake District. Nowadays, they owned and looked after many of the greatest houses in Great Britain and Northern Ireland. One of the first things Ruth had done when she received a lump sum in royalties for a film part had been to become a life member of the National Trust. If she wanted to, she could take Aidan into the castle free of charge. She thought he would be impressed.

"Thought so," he said. His complacency at having summed her up so exactly irritated her. Ruth's romantic tendencies were something she liked to keep well hidden. With annoyance she swished the soapy water with the brush she was holding. "You like nice things, don't you?" he asked.

"In a way. I know what I like." She was unable to resist a smile as she said it. Wasn't that what people always said when they didn't know anything about the fine arts? "I like Melissa Moir's paintings, but nobody else seems to think they're worth much."

"Perhaps not," Aidan mused darkly.

For some reason, his tone of voice made her think of the odd noises she had been hearing round the house recently. If she told him about that, she thought, he would *really* think she had a screw loose.

"Go and sit by the fire and I'll bring some coffee," she commanded him. "With peat fires, you have to watch them every moment or they turn to ash before your very eyes."

"Yes, ma'am," Aidan said, confident he had put his finger on something very important to Ruth Gaynor. She was far from a disappointment to him!

Ruth finished the washing up in a dream. It was a long time since she had liked anyone as much as she did Aidan Wakefield. She didn't pause to consider whether it was liking that she really meant. For the first time in months she felt warm and safe. She even like his bizarre stories of life at the bar. She supposed that, in the end, he saw the whole of life in his profession—as she did in hers, or as much of it as she wanted to.

Aidan was busily feeding the fire when she went back into the sitting room. He still had the guide book clutched under one arm. It wasn't one of hers; few of them were up here. Ruth had browsed through the volumes that were already in the house, marvelling that Miss Moir should have such catholic tastes as to like both Winnie-the-Pooh and Karl Marx, Thomas Aquinas and Regency romances. She had thought some of the books might be valuable. Some of them were leather bound and beautifully illustrated, but what had Melissa Moir been doing with valuable books? The one Aidan had chosen was one of her favourites, too, a beautifully printed copy of the original Lindisfarne Gospels.

Aidan went back to his chair, opening the book to a random page. "Looking at this makes one wonder why we always start our history with 1066 and the Norman Conquest. God, take a look at this, will you?"

She did so, marvelling at the intricacies of the manuscript and the fabled illuminated letters that lay in brilliant reds and blues on the page.

He watched her intently when, after a couple of minutes, she closed the book and restored it to its place in the glass-covered bookcase. She handled the book lovingly. He knew the feeling. There was something wonderful about beautiful books: the smell and the feel of them, as well as the craftsmanship. There was something graceful, too about Ruth's movements that made him feel pleasantly vulnerable. He liked watching her as he couldn't remember liking to watch anyone else, unless it was a gymnast, or a ballerina performing on a stage. It was better than that, though, because he knew and liked Ruth Gaynor...and he meant to know her a whole lot better.

Aidan put some more peat on the fire. She was right about it burning up fast if you didn't watch it. He couldn't think when he had last spent an evening in front of a real fire. It was like having something alive in the room—quite different from the central heating he had at home. This had its own voice, breathing a message of comfort throughout the room. Aidan smiled lazily, wondering how to persuade Ruth to sit on the sofa beside him. He could try telling her she had nothing to fear from him, but he couldn't be certain that that was true. His feelings for her were growing beyond his control.

A scuffling sound brought Aidan to his feet. "What's that?" he demanded.

He wasn't prepared in any way for Ruth's reaction. Ashen-faced, she froze, hunching her shoulders in fear.

"What is it?" he asked again.

"I don't know. I've been telling myself it's my imagination. It happens about the same time every evening." She forced a laugh. "Maybe it's a bird nesting in the chimney. Something is making the fireplace smoke. I ought to have it cleaned out, but I rather like the smell of the burning peat."

"What other noises have you heard?" He dropped the question lightly into the silence as though he already knew the answer. Ruth took the bait at once, her eyes two dark, mysterious pools of fear.

"I think I hear a gun going off in the middle of the night. You know we're being ridiculous, don't you? A couple of townees afraid of perfectly ordinary country noises. Someone born and bred here could tell us what it is and, after a while, we wouldn't even notice it."

He wondered if she really believed that, or if it was something she was telling herself to keep her fears at bay.

"Is that what you've been telling yourself?" he asked her dryly.

She nodded. "You don't believe it?"

"Neither do you," Aidan grunted. He hoped she wasn't thinking what he was thinking. His expression took on a grim aspect as he reviewed the possibilities. However he added it up, the answer remained the same. The noises were harmless in themselves, but were obviously meant as a threat. Ruth was in trouble and it had to be something to do with that "aunt" of hers. An even more uncomfortable thought occurred to him as he recalled the slash on her arm after Jonathan Ross had been killed. Was it possible that Ruth had been the intended victim, not Jonathan?

A slanting glance of enquiry from Ruth made Aidan blink. The last thing he wanted was to add to her fears. He was still recovering from the shock of his thoughts when she said, "All right, Know-all, what do you think it is?"

He stood, thinking about it. "I'm country bred," he said at last. "More or less. I'd have said it sounded like a bird-scarer—you know the sort of thing they put in fields nowadays instead of scarecrows of old," he lied, hoping she would believe him.

"It isn't loud enough for that," Ruth objected.

"No. What about the shots that go off in the middle of the night?"

"They sound as if they come from the field behind the house. I went up to the attic and took a look outside one night, but I was more afraid of coming crashing through the bedroom ceiling than I was of actually seeing anything. There were no lights to be seen, so I backed off downstairs again." She shivered. "I haven't been feeling very brave of late."

"How long have you owned the cottage?"

"Three years. The first year I was waiting for the will to be proved so I never came here. The second year I played the West End and only came up for a couple of weekends in the summer. I don't remember hearing anything then, but I was so tired I probably would have slept through the average earthquake. It's probably only a poacher looking for rabbits, or something like that."

"Rubbish! Why would a poacher come all the way to Lindisfarne?"

"Well, what else can it be?" she asked crossly.

"I don't know," he admitted, "but I've been watching you and you're as nervous as a cat. What else has been happening to you?"

"I don't know. It's also the anonymous calls about the watercolours." She sat down abruptly, as if the power had suddenly gone out of her legs and they refused to support her a minute longer. "Sometimes I think I'm going off my rocker."

In one smooth movement, Aidan scooped her out of her chair and into his arms, holding her tightly against him. "My God," he said. "Nothing will happen to you. I'm here now. Let them do their worst."

"Do you think they might?" she asked in a small voice. "I mean, I could understand it if I were a wealthy heiress, but I'm *nobody*!"

"You're Melissa Moir's heir."

"I've been that for three years. The noises...and the calls...only started recently. Besides, we all know who

Melissa Moir was. She was an old lady who lived on Lindisfarne, making a precarious living from selling her paintings to the summer tourists. Ask anyone.''

''I shall.'' His fingers found the slight scar the slash on her arm had left. ''I wish you'd told me all this before,'' he said. Next she'd be telling him that the noises were all a product of an over-active imagination, but he could tell something very real was frightening her. Over the years, he'd learned to trust his hunches about people's behaviour. Of course, that was in court, when they were more or less at the mercy of his cross-examination. Still, he would be damned if he'd allow anything to happen to Ruth, even if he had to stand guard over her night and day.

Ruth rested her cheek against his shoulder, marvelling at how comfortable it felt to be held by him. ''You must think me an absolute idiot,'' she whispered. ''Just as you did when you first saw me.''

''One day I'll tell you what I really thought of you when I first saw you,'' he promised.

She pushed herself away from him. ''A suitably censored version, I hope?''

He smiled slowly. ''If that's what you want. But I have a feeling that once we got going, we'd be hotter than that fire. How do you feel about it?''

She had no intention of telling him what he was doing to her. She pursed her lips in a prim line, throwing back her head.

And then he kissed her. For a wild moment, Ruth knew it was what she had wanted all along, that she might as well have gone on her knees and begged him for it. She shut her eyes and moaned against his questing mouth. His tongue met hers, exploring her mouth with an intimacy that both shocked and inspired her.

She clutched at his shoulder when he moved away, her knees buckling beneath her. Never in her wildest dreams had she imagined that anyone could have such an effect on her. Who would believe she had reached thirty, had been kissed a hundred times on the stage, and had never known the first thing about love? What a simpleton he must think her.

"I'd better go," Aidan said gently. He ran a casual finger down her nose, smiling at her. "I don't think you're ready for what I'd really like to do with you. I'm staying next door with the Jenkinses, as a matter of fact. If you should hear any bangs in the night," he added, half-hopefully, "you've only got to cry out and I'll be right here!"

"You haven't got a key," she pointed out, and winced at her words. Other women could think of delightful, romantic things to say when a man kissed them good-night. Why did she have to be maddeningly practical?

"Are you going to give me one?" Aidan said, trying to convince himself he wanted it for her protection.

Ruth nodded, unable to say anything at all. It took her some time to find the spare key and to test it in the front door. All the time she was aware of his eyes watching her every movement. She didn't have to turn her head to remind herself of a single detail of the way he looked. Aidan Wakefield would be imprinted on her mind forever. And her body? Ruth's face was hot when she finally handed him the key.

"I shan't need to call you," she said. "I've taken to pulling the bedclothes up over my head—"

"Are you afraid of the dark, too?"

Too? Was *he* afraid of the dark? The thought made her laugh. "Certainly not!" she said.

The cottage felt cold and empty after he had gone. Ruth had been alone all of her life and that was the way she had liked it. It would be a fine thing if she were to come un-glued merely because some man had kissed her and had now gone away to sleep next door. She rubbed her hands down her skirt uneasily, wishing she hadn't told him her secret fears. She put the guard in front of the remains of the fire and went up to bed. One way and another, Aidan Wake-field was proving a totally new experience for her—and she wasn't at all sure whether she should trust him or not.

Chapter Four

The bleep of the telephone aroused Ruth from sleep. For an instant she wondered what on earth the time was. Then she wondered who could be phoning her at the cottage. She'd had the telephone installed a few weeks before in case Judith needed to get in touch with her, but she had made sure that the number was ex-directory. She'd had more than enough of the inquisitive tabloid press to last her a lifetime, and she certainly hadn't wanted them following her to her retreat and making her an object of speculation among her neighbours.

Ruth picked up the receiver. "Yes?" she said tentatively.

It wasn't Judith. Or anyone she knew. "I knew Melissa Moir," the disembodied voice announced flatly.

"Did you now?" Ruth said. It was possible, she supposed, though not likely. This man sounded far too young to fit with Ruth's picture of her benefactress.

"We go way back," the voice went on. "I wondered if any of her paintings were still in the cottage? Before she died, she promised me first pick, as it were—"

"And it's taken you three years to get around to asking about them? You *are* keen, Mr—?"

"Has it really been three years? It seems like yesterday," the voice went on in mock sadness. "As a matter of fact, I did try to get in touch before but the cottage seemed to be empty, and none of the villagers knew anything about the new owner. I'm glad to know you've finally moved in."

Ruth stirred uneasily. It all could be true, but a prickly feeling on the back of her neck told her not to believe a word of it. "What about the paintings?" she asked.

"I have a sentimental interest in them. Melissa was never much good, bless her heart, but I kind of like them and she did promise them to me. I'll give you a few bob for them, so we'll both be the gainers."

"I kind of like them myself," Ruth said.

"You do? Well, I don't mind if you hang on to one or two of them. I don't suppose you have room for many of them really. Where are they now? Stowed away in some cupboard somewhere?"

Ruth took a grip on herself. "Is that any of your business?"

"Sure it is. Painting is my business."

"Then why don't you write me a letter about all this, telling me who you are and everything else, and I'll think about it."

The man laughed. "That sounds all right, but I don't come all the way up here often. That's another reason why you haven't heard from me before. How many paintings have you got?"

The man was here in Lindisfarne! Ruth wished Aidan was on hand to help quell her fears. "I'm not telling you anything over the phone," she said keeping her voice firm. "I don't know anything about you—"

"I'm not trying to steal anything from you."

"I think you'll have to tell me a lot more about yourself than *that*!" Ruth nearly shouted.

"You can tell me how many of her paintings you have?" the man wheedled. "Where's the harm in that?"

"I've said all I've got to say," she answered. "You haven't told me your name—"

She heard a sharp click. He'd slammed the receiver down. Ruth stared at her telephone in shock, listening to the dial tone, which frightened her as it never had before. *How had he got her number?*

Glancing at her watch, Ruth saw it was too late to turn over and go back to sleep, even if she could have. She lay back briefly, wondering where the night had gone. She had slept the whole night through and that was for the first time since she couldn't remember when. There had been no odd noises to keep her awake, nothing but the warm, snug feeling that Aidan had engendered. She thought again of the telephone call that had awakened her. There was no doubt about it, the unknown man had left an uncomfortable feeling behind him. What had he really wanted? And what did Aidan Wakefield want? Today, she meant to find out.

Ruth had developed a technique that she went through just before she went onstage. When she had finished making up and was sure her costume was right, she would sit in front of her mirror for a few minutes and consciously put on the character she was playing, much as she had dressed herself, first the underclothes and then the outer garments. Sometimes, as she went through the routine, she could feel her features changing to fit the mannerisms and habits of the other woman. Putting on her skin, she called it. Then she would shut her eyes and breathe deeply once or twice, forc-

ing herself to relax. After that she felt ready for anything—
she was the part she was playing and no longer herself.

Ruth thrust her feet into her slippers and opened up her
wardrobe, looking over her clothes with a thoughtful air.
Nothing too smart, she decided. A pair of jeans, a shirt that
looked as if it were made of silk but was really a man-made,
drip-dry material and a striped waistcoat in pinks and greys
that wasn't really country gear, but which looked all right no
matter what the circumstances.

Once dressed, she looked at herself in the glass and saw a
stranger. Her stubborn chin and generous mouth be-
tokened a more emotional kind of person than she had ever
been. She decided she'd concentrate on the stubborn chin
and the distant look, as if nothing was quite real to her. She
couldn't afford to be emotional just now, any more than she
could afford to be too trusting. *Why had Aidan followed her
north? That telephone call certainly hadn't been a figment
of her imagination!*

Halfway down the stairs, she smelt the brewing coffee and
the bacon frying. The last time anyone had made breakfast
for her had been when she was sixteen. Ruth felt quite
overwhelmed to think Aidan had let himself into her house
and had set to all by himself, without even calling out to her,
or hanging around until she was ready to make breakfast for
them both as most men would. He certainly was unusual.
She stood in the kitchen doorway, watching him work as she
tried to rediscover the hard shell she thought she had successfully donned upstairs. She felt shy and vulnerable and
that, she told herself severely, she couldn't afford to be!

"Good morning," Ruth said, trying to keep her tone
stern.

He smiled at her over his shoulder. "Hungry?"

She nodded, surprised to discover that she was. Suddenly, his cheerful smile melted her apprehension. "I can see you're going to eat me out of house and home," she joked.

"Don't worry about it. There are a couple of shops round the corner and presumably one of them will sell us something to eat."

"Mmm," she said thoughtfully.

"Meaning what?"

"One of them sells crab sandwiches. We could buy a couple of packets and take them with us to eat on the beach, or wherever."

He gave her a pleased smile. "You're on! I'll buy the sandwiches and the drink and everything, and you can carry it!"

"We'll take the car," she decided. "We can park it down by the Snook and walk along the North Shore."

"Okay," he agreed. "You're the boss."

"Remember that," she advised him. "This is my backyard, Aidan, and I don't want it spoiled for me."

Noting her serious tone of voice, he hesitated in the midst of cracking an egg over the frying pan. "Could I spoil it for you?"

"N—no. I just wish I knew why you came, that's all."

The egg splattered and crackled in the hot fat. Ruth took one look at Aidan's pensive expression and whisked the spatula out of his hand, turning the heat down and pushing the egg round to prevent its edges from burning.

"You really *don't* know, do you?" he said.

"It's a long way to come just to see someone. What do you want from me?"

He shook his head at her. "*Hinny*, where've you been all your life? I like you. I want to get to know you better. Men have been known to go a good deal farther than a few hundred miles for a lot less."

She gave him a wry look. "Don't tell me you can't find all you want in London. You've never lacked for female company, Aidan. I knew that much about you the first time I set eyes on you."

His eyes crinkled at the corners. "That's the first bit of encouragement you've given me so far, love. Keep it up."

She was immediately indignant. "I was merely stating a fact."

"Oh, don't go and spoil it. Where you're concerned, I have an ambition to be the most attractive man in the world." He sat down at the table, waiting for her to put his breakfast on a plate. "How did you come to be so shy?" he asked her. "You can't have reached your age without having gained some experience of falling in love."

She plonked the plate down in front of him, breaking her own egg into the pan without answering. The truth was that she didn't know what to say. She didn't think he'd believe that she'd always been too busy. She hardly believed it herself. Nor did she want to tell him how frightened she had been when she had first arrived in London, her ears ringing with the stories of what happened to young girls on their own.

Her social worker had looked down her nose when Ruth had told her of her ambitions, convinced she was heading straight for disaster. Either she would end up a victim of white slavery, or drugs, or worse! Actually, Ruth had fallen on her feet almost immediately. She'd found a room in the house of a religious-minded spinster who had watched over her with all the devotion of an anxious sheepdog, declaring that sixteen was far too young for any person to be responsible for herself.

"Of course you think you're old enough," the woman had said in that funny, brusque way she had of speaking, "but you're not, no matter if every politician in the land has decided you are. Whilst you're under my roof, you will bring your friends home and introduce them to me before you accept any invitations. You won't like it, I daresay, but you'll thank me later on.''

Ruth had been thankful for her interest then and there. She had lodged with the old lady right up until the woman had taken ill and had reluctantly gone off to live with a niece in the West Country. Then Ruth had been lost without her kindly interest. She had never trusted her own judgment when it came to men, nor had she wasted much time regretting her lack of a social life. Having been orphaned at a very young age, Ruth was accustomed to being alone. She hadn't noticed the lack until now.

She carried her full plate over to the table and sat down opposite Aidan. She never ate a cooked breakfast, so what was she doing with one now? She poured herself a cup of coffee, trying to persuade herself there weren't as many calories in fried bacon and eggs as she knew there were.

"Do you eat like this all the time?" she asked Aidan with distaste.

"I don't have time usually." His gaze swept up and held hers. "From the look of you, you don't eat enough to keep body and soul together."

"I keep fit and healthy. You have to be both in my job."

She could tell he wasn't taking her too seriously about that. Many people didn't. But she planned to show him exactly how fit she was. By the time she'd finished walking Aidan around Lindisfarne, he'd be crying out for a rest!

Ruth washed the few breakfast things while Aidan went off into the village and bought their lunch. By the time he had returned she'd backed her car out onto the road and was waiting for him, seated firmly in the driver's seat. He didn't say a word, but he looked volumes.

Folding himself into the passenger seat beside her, Aidan gave her a knowing grin. "You're determined to show me this is your patch, aren't you?"

Ruth's eyes were serious, almost grave, as she regarded him in silence for a long moment. "I still don't know what you're doing here," she said at last. "Until I know that, I'm not taking any chances. Do you blame me?"

"I doubt I'd ever blame you for anything. I have the feeling, though, that you're pushing me into playing a part for which I haven't seen the script—"

"What do you know of Melissa Moir?" she interrupted him.

"What you've told me about her, nothing more."

She wrinkled her brow, setting the car in motion. "Nothing about her seems to make sense," she said.

"I imagine the locals know all there is to know about her. Why don't you ask them?"

She sighed. "What makes you think I haven't?"

"What makes you think there's anything to know?"

"I don't know," she admitted.

"Woman's intuition?"

Ruth reddened, suspecting a sneer in his voice that she couldn't actually hear. "What's wrong with that?" she demanded.

He brushed her cheek with his forefinger, giving her such a start that they nearly left the road. "Nothing," he said. "I just wish you didn't feel you have to hide what you're really thinking from me. There haven't been many troubles halved in your life, have there?"

"I've yet to have it proved to me that a trouble shared is necessarily halved in the first place," she answered cautiously.

Aidan brushed her cheek again. "Why don't you try it?"

Ruth couldn't answer. She took the road that led to the Snook, the westerly part of the island, which was largely made up of sand dunes and rabbit warrens. She parked the car and got out quickly, pulling her anorak closer about her as she felt the freshness of the wind.

"If you can walk as well as you talk, I'll tell you all I know about Melissa Moir over lunch," she promised.

"You're on!"

His legs were much stronger than hers and he was over the bank and already striding along the shore before Ruth had gathered her wits together. Damn the man! She hadn't wanted to turn their walk into a race. She loved this part of the island and liked to stop and gaze, savouring the stark beauty of the wild, windblown area. She liked to stand still enough for the rabbits to come out and scurry about their business only a few yards from her feet.

Ruth followed Aidan along the rough path to the sands, deliberately taking her time. He was out of sight for a moment or so, and then she saw him, hands on hips, staring out to sea, his back to her. The picture he made took her breath away. She was merely being foolish if she thought she could spend much more time with him and remain indifferent. She wasn't sure that he hadn't already undermined her defences—but no, she couldn't allow that! She still didn't know what he was doing here and, until she did know, she couldn't allow herself to get sentimental over him, or anything else. Why did the thought upset her so? She tried to put the feeling of devastation away from her as she ran the last few yards.

"Sometimes one can see seals from this beach," she told him. "We might see them at Snipe Point. Sometimes they come ashore there."

"I can see why you like it up here," Aidan said. "It's a long way from London and the rat-race, isn't it?"

Ruth only nodded. People who had been born and bred up north frequently had to go south to find work, but they usually left their hearts behind them.

"Isn't this Grace Darling country?" he went on.

"Oh, yes, she's very much the local heroine. The Longstone Lighthouse, where her father worked, adopted an orphan seal recently, and even though it's now quite grown-up, it still goes back for a free meal from the keepers whenever it can."

"I didn't realise her father was the lighthouse keeper at the Longstone," he said.

"Mmm, it was from there that Grace saw the *Forfarshire* foundering on the Big Harcar Rock, half a mile out at sea. When she saw some movements on the rock, she persuaded her father to take a lifeboat out despite the high seas that were whipped up all around them. With her mother's help, she and her father manhandled the twenty-foot boat across the island to Sunderland Hole, which was sheltered enough from the storm for them to launch it safely. From there, she and her father rowed out twice to the rock, bringing off all the survivors, eight men and a woman. The Victorians took her to their hearts, as you may imagine, and raised eight hundred pounds by public subscription in appreciation of her heroic act."

"You seem to know quite a bit about her."

"Of course. I can't think how often I played Grace Darling at school. She was my first starring part. I took my thespian activities very seriously in those days."

"And now?"

"I still do," she sighed. "It's the only security I've ever known." She laughed to dispel the seriousness of her statement. "I'd have done better to have become a shorthand typist, wouldn't I? Regular money every month to pay the regular bills that keep coming in."

"There's more to life than paying bills."

Her look was pure mockery. "There speaks someone who never had to worry where the next meal was coming from."

"What makes you think that?"

"It's written all over you." Ruth paused to rest, chagrined to discover that he seemed as eager to press on as ever. Her mockery turned to petulance. "I'm going to sit down for a while."

"All right," Aidan said, noting with amusement Ruth's dismay at being outlasted. He unstrapped the ground sheet he was wearing over one shoulder and spread it out on the rocks. "It would make my day if we saw some seals," he said.

Ruth sat on the groundsheet with relief, glad to get off her feet. The sun was pleasantly warm despite the wind, and the sea crashed soothingly. She leaned back, closing her eyes, trying not to think about the morning's phone call. Had Aidan had anything to do with that? She very much hoped not.

When Ruth opened her eyes again, she saw him standing right out on the point, scanning the seas for the seals. She thought he looked magnificent, a powerful grace in the set of his shoulders. It had been mean of her to tease him because he had a few bob and she hadn't earned a penny in weeks. It wasn't his fault if she had money worries.

She was almost asleep again when he came back to her. He sat down beside her, his smooth movements giving her a conscious pleasure, such as one received from watching a dance step well performed. She felt a special jolt of pleasure when he leaned over and pushed a lock of her hair away from her face.

"There are some seals out there," he said so quietly she had to strain her ears to hear him. "If we stay quiet and still they may feel brave enough to come ashore."

His pleasure rubbed off on her and her eyes were warm and welcoming as he settled down beside her.

"They don't like human beings littering up their rocks," she warned him. "I saw some boys throwing stones at them the other day. They don't see us at our best, I'm afraid."

"Hush," he said.

Her reaction to having him so close beside her reached her toes and she wiggled them thoughtfully in her sensible shoes. If he were to kiss her now—

A great, lumbering bull seal heaved itself out of the water, sniffing the air suspiciously. If the odour of the hated enemy came to its nostrils, it gave no sign. It looked in their direction several times, its whiskers quivering, but Ruth didn't believe it could really see them. After a while, it heaved up onto the rocks, easing its body into a familiar spot where it could sunbathe at peace.

Ruth watched the females pull themselves up onto the point, one by one, staying well away from the irascible old bull. Using one another's stomachs to pillow their heads, they were soon fast asleep, only the occasional yawning movement distinguishing them from the rocks on which they lay.

"Atlantic seals," Ruth said under her breath.

Aidan put an arm about her shoulders, hugging her close against his chest. "This is the life, isn't it?"

She would have agreed if she could have been sure that he meant it. She wished the doubt in her mind would go away, but it was still there, no matter how hard she tried to banish it. She couldn't believe that he had come all this way just to see her. Why would he? Ruth moved cautiously away from him, only to come up against the barrier of his arm. Casting him a swift look, she saw he wasn't watching the seals at all. The tender enquiry in his eyes brought the heat rushing into her face. *She could fall in love with this man! What was she going to do?*

Ruth tried to look away, but she couldn't. She was drowning in his dark, sympathetic eyes. It was easy to believe that this man really liked her, perhaps had even warmer feelings for her, but why should he have fallen in love with her?

She swallowed. "Some people think seals and human beings are quite closely related," she said, trying to distract both Aidan and herself.

"What makes them think that?"

"Something to do with the blood," she answered. She thought it had to do with the amount of saline in the blood, but she couldn't really remember. And looking at this man was rendering her incapable of much thought at all!

He kissed the tip of her nose. "You have a prettier face than a seal—a prettier face than any woman I can think of."

"Thank you, kind sir."

A muscle pulsed in his cheek. "Kindness has nothing to do with it."

She made her face expressionless. "Oh?"

He was immediately impatient. "I wish I knew what you're thinking, deep down in here." He touched her over her heart. "You're a good actress, Ruth Gaynor. Sometimes I catch a glimpse of the vulnerable woman underneath, but you don't want me to know about her, do you?"

She shook her head, her eyes downcast. "No."

"Why not?"

"I don't know what you want from me."

He had more going for him than he knew, though, she thought bitterly. Her breasts had tightened at his touch, ready and eager for his caress. She felt like a finely tuned musical instrument, a violin awaiting the touch of the bow to be brought into a new, pulsating life. It wouldn't do.

"Still suspicious?"

His eyes narrowed dangerously. He didn't like not getting his own way, she reflected. That was probably why he was good at his job. He didn't believe in letting sleeping dogs lie. "Shouldn't I be?" Ruth said.

"I'd rather you thought you could trust me. Why don't you?"

"I don't know." She sat up, seeking to destroy the spell he was weaving about her. It was a forlorn hope. She had only to shut her eyes to see the elegance of his strong hands, and to long for them against her naked skin. "I think we ought to be going back to the car," she said.

He smiled at her. "The seals will be disappointed."

She raised her brows. "Because we're going?"

"Because they won't witness how nicely I was going to kiss you," he retorted.

He went on muttering, but the only words she could make out were "highly educational." It would have been an education for her, too, she thought, and wondered how she knew. She would almost have liked to snuggle back beside him, just for a few minutes, just until she could be sure she was doing the right thing in rejecting him—as if she didn't know that already.

Ruth got to her feet in a single, easy movement, nudging him with her toe. "Last one back to the car is a rotten egg," she challenged.

He captured her foot in one hand. "You do like to live dangerously don't you, my love? Who had a hard job keeping up with me on the way out?"

So he had noticed, had he? She made a face at him. "Your legs are longer than mine," she said.

He stood up also. "I'll give you a decent start," he offered. "If I still beat you to the car, I choose the forfeit you must pay me. How's that?"

Ruth felt the laughter bubbling somewhere in her middle as she accepted the challenge. "I'll need at least a hundred yards' start!"

"Start walking," he commanded.

Ruth chose a bleached tree that had been washed up on the beach at least two hundred yards from where they were standing. "When I reach that, you can start to follow."

When she reached the tree, she saw he was still standing where she had left him, watching the sway of her hips as she idled her way along, making the most of her advantage. She broke into a run as she came level with the dead wood, laughing at him. He went on standing there, looking at her, his hands on his hips. Her laughter died. She almost missed her footing and still he didn't move. Didn't he want to win his bet?

She must have covered another hundred yards at least before he began to come after her. She had stopped running, choosing instead to cover the sands with an easy, rhythmic stride, not daring to look back again, but concentrating on getting there first as if her whole life depended on it. How had she ever gotten herself into this?

Aidan passed her when she was scarcely five yards away from the car. He wasn't even breathing heavily. She could have screamed when she saw the smile on his face. How dared he laugh at her!

He reached out for her, the jut of his chin more determined than she had yet seen it. "My forfeit, I think!" he said triumphantly.

"Okay, I don't mind cooking dinner tonight," she said, hoping to put him off.

His hand cupped her chin, raising her face to his. "Who said anything about cooking?" he demanded.

"Wasn't that the forfeit you had in mind?"

"No, Miss Innocent, it was not." Aidan grinned slowly. She was unable to hide from him the fleeting anxiety that lay behind her cool exterior. "You knew I meant to kiss you sooner or later. You want it as much as I do. Wasn't that what this whole charade was about?"

Her eyes flashed. "I beg your pardon!"

"It would be nice, sometimes, not to have to say no, wouldn't it?"

Ruth spluttered between laughter and indignation. "Perhaps," she admitted. There was a look in his eyes that made her mouth go dry and her toes curl in her shoes.

"You know," he said slowly, "you're a darling when you're not hiding behind the whole acting profession. That's why I want to kiss you."

"Oh," she said.

"Yes, oh," he agreed smugly.

And then he kissed her.

Chapter Five

Aidan didn't kiss Ruth again that day, and, much as she wanted to deny it, his explanation was rather less than satisfactory to her.

"I need all the allies I can muster when I take you on," he had told her. "The fact that you like my kisses is my best weapon. I don't mean to squander it, *hinny*, not while the last encounter is working in your mind to my advantage."

Aidan had been laughing when he spoke. Ruth had never felt less like laughing in her life. The thing that annoyed her most of all was that he was quite right in his assessment of her reaction. She was haunted by the memory of the touch and taste of him. It was there with her all the time—and not only in her waking moments when she could fight back. He had taken over her dreams as well!

"What's the point of it all?" she had asked him.

"We can't have you gathering dust on a shelf forever!" he had replied gravely.

"What business is that of yours?"

"Let's just say I don't fancy dusty shelves myself," he had observed with such gentle tolerance that she felt as though she had made some sort of social gaffe. Which was why, when he suggested she accompany him to Durham to meet his parents, she refused with quite unnecessary vigour, telling herself she would be glad to see the back of him for a while.

That was yesterday. Ruth wasn't quite so sure of herself now that today yawned endlessly ahead of her and she had to face up to it all alone. She had spent a restless, disturbed night, imagining people breaking into the house, and having to get up several times to reassure herself that all the doors and the downstairs windows were securely locked and bolted.

She'd awoken with a headache and a determination to search the whole property in case she had overlooked anything when she had sent all Melissa Moir's private papers to her lawyer. Ruth had no idea of what she was looking for, but it would give her something to do. After looking with mounting disbelief at all the junk that had been pushed into the cupboard under the stairs during more years than she had been alive, she emerged to notice that one of the Melissa Moir watercolours was missing from its usual place in the hall.

She stared, hypnotized by the square of unfaded wallpaper, which was the only evidence that anything had ever hung there. The wallpaper, now a neutral shade of brown and grey, had been a vivid mix of blue and green. If she hadn't known better, Ruth would have thought the stuff terribly expensive. She ran her fingers lightly over the patch of wall and marvelled at the silky texture. Nobody she knew could afford to hang silk on their walls these days.

Melissa Moir was becoming more interesting by the minute. If Ruth cast her mind back to the day her parents died, she could just barely remember a shadowy figure who had looked down at her from a great height and had finally said to her: "Well, Ruth Gaynor, it looks as though we're stuck with one another. Unless you have some other plan in mind, you'd better come and live with me."

Other people had mentioned the social services once it had been established that Ruth had no living relatives. Miss Moir claimed that Ruth's parents would have wanted her to be Ruth's guardian and had ignored them, taking Ruth by the hand and smiling at her for the first time.

"You might say I'm related to you," she had told the tearful little girl. "We share a grandfather in Adam, and a grandmother in Eve."

Little Ruth had never heard of either of them, but then she had never heard of Miss Moir, either.

"What's your name?" she had asked.

"Miss Moir."

In the days that followed, somebody had taken it upon himself to suggest to Ruth she might call the tall lady Aunt Melissa.

"Aunt M'lissa," Ruth had obliged.

Miss Moir had recoiled from the familiarity. "Never call me that again," she had said firmly.

Ruth never had. Not that she had lived with Miss Moir for longer than a few months, before a social worker, designated "that interfering female" by Miss Moir, had duly arrived on the scene and had put an end to the most interesting period of Ruth's life by removing her to a children's home in Berwick. Many years later, when Ruth had been allowed to see her file before leaving the care of the social services forever, she had discovered that Miss Moir had done everything she could to keep Ruth with her.

Miss Gaynor is a friend of mine, the woman had written. *I consider her to be in greater need of her friends than all the benefits the state can shower on her. Her schooling is quite incidental to the life I propose to share with her.* It had come as no surprise to anyone that her offer had been refused in stinging terms. It had warmed Ruth's heart, however, ten years after the letter had been written, to see herself referred to as Miss Gaynor, and not as "the child Ruth," or as a "ward of the state." It might have been interesting at that to have been brought up by someone of Miss Moir's unusual quality. Ruth wished she had known her better.

Still, none of that explained where the missing painting was now, nor who could have taken it. A shudder went through Ruth's body as she remembered the sounds she had heard in the night. Had someone managed to break in after all?

She was reluctant to call the police, but she didn't see that she had any choice. The tides were wrong for them to come immediately, the officer told her, unless she wanted them to come by boat. Ruth replied that she didn't. She couldn't see what they could do anyway. It wasn't as if it were a valuable painting. It had just happened to be one of her favourites, showing the view out the back door, with the harbour and the castle in the background.

Ruth refused to admit to herself that she was frightened. She had never had a break-in, even in her various flats in town. It wasn't long before she decided to go out—anything rather than remain indoors brooding over the painting's disappearance. She would walk over to the castle, she thought. Or she might visit Mrs. Jenkins, who had called on her a couple of days ago, expressing her characteristic concern for her neighbours.

"Never did understand why Miss Moir couldn't have you live with her! If you'd agreed to it, what business was it of anyone else?" Mrs. Jenkins had said.

She was still the large, warmhearted woman Ruth re-membered. "Children are people, too," Ruth had agreed, almost wistfully.

Then Mrs. Jenkins had said a most remarkable thing about Miss Moir. "More money than sense," she had ob-served, her eyes twinkling. "Come and see us sometime, my dear, and tell us how you like living in Miss Moir's house. Not going to sell up, are you?"

Ruth had been quite firm about that and Mrs. Jenkins had looked relieved.

Now Ruth was going out the door when she saw Aidan's note. Snatching it up, she ripped it open, knowing, even as she did so, who had removed the painting from the hall-way. Blind fury at his forward action was followed by relief that no one had broken in, after all. She was still trembling with indignation, however, when she rang the police again to tell them not to come. They didn't even sound surprised when she offered her lame explanation as to why they weren't needed, despite her earlier panicky demands that they should come at once. By the time they had finished patronizing her with their assurances that this happened to them all the time and that they didn't set too much store by such incidents, she was fuming and more than ready to tell Aidan a thing or two about what she thought of his remov-ing her property without bothering to tell her about it.

She was halfway to the castle before she wondered why Aidan had wanted her painting, anyway. Could his actions be linked to her anonymous caller? It gave her a creepy feeling to think about the calls. Aidan had had plenty of opportunity to tell her he was taking the painting, so why come into her house in the middle of the night to get it? If he had wanted to steal it, she supposed, he wouldn't have left a note, but why take it in the first place? *Who was Ai-dan Wakefield? And what did he really want?*

For the first time, the visit to Lindisfarne Castle failed to soothe Ruth. She forced herself to mount the outside steps, turning back at one point, as she always did, to gaze at the sheds that had been made from some old boat hulls—fantastic, pleasing shapes that Melissa Moir had frequently painted. When Ruth at last gained entrance to the castle, she showed her membership card and trailed round the beautifully refurbished rooms, wondering why she was getting so little pleasure from Lutyens's work, when usually she felt only a great satisfaction that the architect who had drawn the plans for New Delhi in India had also brought his skills to bear on a tiny, unknown castle, miles from anywhere.

For the most part, Ruth was alone as she made her tour of the steeply vaulted rooms, forcing herself to observe how the windows were set in deep embrasures. She got as far as the dining room before she acknowledged to herself that she was bored and lonely—and afraid! She could tell herself all day she had nothing to be afraid of, but it wasn't making any difference. She could still feel a tremor of fear somewhere in her middle whenever she tried to relax and forget about the whole business.

Ruth glanced at her watch and realized she would miss the tide unless she ran. She took to her heels, hoping none of the castle attendants recognized her from town. How had the time gotten away from her?

The car park was empty. Two boys were doing handstands against the wall that marked the perimeter of the castle grounds. They called out to her, recognizing her as a local.

"The wind's changing, miss. Don't you go walking down by the causeway," one of the boys shouted.

Ruth grinned at him. She could barely remember her mother saying exactly the same to her as a child, but she recognized the parental concern echoed in the young voices. "I won't," she promised.

Mrs. Jenkins's door was standing open to the street. Ruth knocked, calling the woman's name.

"It's Ruth Gaynor," she said, leaning through the doorway.

Mrs. Jenkins came bustling out to greet her. "I was beginning to wonder if you were ever coming," she said with northern frankness. "Neighbours don't visit much down in London, I'm told."

"No, they don't. Most people keep themselves to themselves."

Mrs. Jenkins muttered something uncomplimentary about city dwellers in general and Londoners in particular. "Don't know they're alive down there, they don't," she added for good measure.

Ruth's eyes sparkled. "They think the same about us," she said.

"I wouldn't live in London, not if you paid me to. Still, I suppose you're used to their goings-on by now, though you must be glad to come home for a breath of fresh air every now and then."

Ruth nodded. "Miss Moir's house—"

"She always said she'd leave it to you," Mrs. Jenkins interrupted, leading the way into the kitchen where she was busy baking a generous loaf of bread. "Sit yourself down, my dear, and I'll make us a cup of tea as soon as I've got the bread into the oven. I expect you could do with a loaf? Nothing like home-baked bread, is there?"

"I'm not much of a cook," Ruth admitted.

"You'll learn. You've little else to do with your time just now, have you?"

Ruth gave her a long, level look. "You know about that, do you?"

"I read the newspapers and watch the television, just like everyone else. That doesn't mean I believe it all, so there's no need to look so hangdog. What would you be doing killing a man you'd never even met?"

"I could have been carrying on with him behind his wife's back."

"And you a Gaynor? Don't talk daft, girl! Your mother'd have had something to say to you if she knew how you'd got yourself talked about down there! Let alone Miss Moir! *She* wouldn't have allowed them to put you in prison—"

Ruth started at the thought that this woman might be able to tell her about her parents, but she wanted to defend herself to Mrs. Jenkins's disapproval. "It was only while they sorted things out. They let me go as soon as they realized they hadn't got a case against me."

Mrs. Jenkins sniffed. "Prison is prison. Where has that young man of yours gone?"

Ruth helped herself from the plate of homemade pastries on the table. "He's gone to visit his parents."

"Why didn't he take you with him?"

"He wanted to—"

"But you can't make up your mind about him? Never did know what you wanted, did you? Funny little girl you were, settling into Miss Moir's house as if it were the only place in the world for you. Maybe it wasn't suitable, with her being a single lady and all, but you could have done worse. There was a lot more to Miss Moir than most people knew!"

"I can hardly remember her," Ruth confessed. "She was very tall, wasn't she?"

"Tall, and as thin as a broomstick. We always used to say the wind never noticed her, sitting out there in all weathers, painting away. It was the breath of life to her."

Ruth finished her pastry. "That's what I wanted to ask you about," she said. "What did Miss Moir do with all her paintings? She couldn't have made much of a living selling them to passing tourists—"

"Lord bless you, no! You're as bad as the rest of them, thinking that just because Lindisfarne isn't London we don't have a mite of talent among us. We've had more than our share of artists, going right back to the monks who illustrated the gospels in Cuthbert's memory. Haven't you seen St. Aidan's statue outside the priory? Or looked at the altar rug in the parish church? You won't find anything finer down south and don't you think it!"

"You mean Miss Moir was famous?"

"No, I don't mean that. Miss Moir was Miss Moir. It was her paintings that were famous. They used to ask her to make personal appearances as far away as America, but she never went. Never wanted to. Once or twice, one of her relations would turn up and try to act as her business manager. She'd never allow them over the threshold." Mrs. Jenkins laughed at the memory. "That woman had more bank accounts than Ali Baba had jewels. She wasn't going to have anyone messing in her financial affairs, yet she knew to the nearest penny what she was worth, and she knew exactly what she was going to do with it. She left it in her will that her relations weren't to be told of her death when she died. As far as I know, they weren't."

"They know now," Ruth said, digesting this new information. She couldn't have said why she was so certain about it, but she could well imagine that they were the source of her trouble.

Mrs. Jenkins gave her a sharp look. "If you'll take my advice, you won't get involved, my dear. I'll say this for Miss Moir, she was always an excellent judge of character. If she didn't want them anywhere near her, you can be sure there was a very good reason for it."

Ruth rubbed the scar on her arm without knowing she was doing so. "I wish you'd tell me about her. I hardly remember her. You knew my parents too, didn't you? I know so little about them."

"Aye, I knew them. I remember them coming here when they were newlywed. Your father thought he'd earn a living helping out round the castle and writing a few historical essays in his spare time. It hadn't occurred to him that the more highbrow the journal the less they pay—stands to reason, doesn't it, when they can get any number of contributors ready to write them for the honour of seeing their names in print. No, it was your mother who set to and earned a living for the three of you by designing knitting patterns, and doing a bit of spinning and weaving on the side. Very clever at that sort of thing she was. I expect you're good with your needle, too."

Ruth shook her head with a rueful smile. "I can barely thread a needle," she confessed.

"I suppose you were too young to have been taught by your mother before they both were drowned," Mrs. Jenkins said placidly. "What did they teach you in that home they put you in?"

"I went to a good school—"

"Did you now? And what made you think you'd like to be an actress?" Ruth's astonished look made the other woman laugh. "We have television on Lindisfarne. I might not have recognized you myself, I have to admit, but Miss Moir did. Came running over here, she did, the first play you did on television, saying 'Our Miss Gaynor is on the box! I think we can be proud of our Miss Gaynor!' she used to say. It was seeing you on the telly that made me know who you were when you started living in Miss Moir's cottage."

Ruth's eyes misted. "Did she really still call me Miss Gaynor?"

"Never called you anything else."

"I loved her for that when I was a small child."

"Made you feel grown-up, I expect. She was ever a stickler for formality, that one. I must be known by my Christian name to all and sundry on the island, but she never called me anything other than Mrs. Jenkins, and I was the closest she came to having a friend here. I won't say she wasn't strange, for she was, but I liked her."

"I did too. I hated being taken away from her," Ruth said sadly.

Mrs. Jenkins heaved a sigh. "Ay, it was a sad day for her and no mistake, but it was probably just as well for you. She'd have made you as eccentric and lonely as she was herself, I have no doubt—"

"I only remember her as being kind."

Mrs. Jenkins's eyes laughed at Ruth over the table. "You don't have to defend her to *me!* Her family didn't know her as I did, however."

"Have you met any of them?"

"There was a young woman who came sniffing around, making enquiries about the cottage. She wanted me to let her in so she could have a look, but I reckoned that she could call Miss Moir 'Auntie Lissa' all she liked—it didn't mean she'd ever met her. Since the day she died, I've never let a soul through that door, just as her lawyers said. I would have sent them the key Miss Moir gave me in case she ever locked herself out long ago, but to tell you the truth, I forgot I had it. And then I heard she'd left you the cottage, and

I thought I might as well hang on to it, in case you ever wanted any groceries got in sometime. I can give it to you now, if you like."

Ruth reminded herself she was living in the country now, where nobody every locked his door except at night, and where the precautions of the city probably seemed ridiculous. She knew, too, she would offend Mrs. Jenkins beyond forgiveness if she were to snatch it back now, especially as the only excuse she could offer wouldn't have deceived a child. Who would believe her if she said she was afraid of what might happen to her on Lindisfarne—where nothing had happened since the last Viking raid kept the local population hiding out in their homes.

"I'm glad to know you have it," Ruth compromised. "If Miss Moir gave it to you—"

"I keep several keys," Mrs. Jenkins said. "I'll show it to you anyway, and then you can make up your mind about it."

Ruth wondered how seeing the key, which probably looked like a hundred others, was supposed to be of any interest to her. Slightly resentful at having to stir out of the comfortable kitchen, which reminded her obscurely of a childhood she thought she had completely forgotten, Ruth followed her hostess out to the back door. There was a whole row of keys hanging on nails, all of them in full sight of anyone who stood in the open doorway. Ruth shuddered to think what any security firm would have made of such casual arrangements. It was a wonder anyone on Lindisfarne could get insurance at all.

"That's odd," Mrs. Jenkins said.

"What's odd?"

"Your key isn't here, dear."

Ruth wasn't surprised. Mrs. Jenkins probably hadn't used it in years. "It doesn't matter," she said. "I'll have the locks changed."

The contemptuous look she received made her realize she had said the wrong thing.

"Whatever would you do that for?" Mrs. Jenkins enquired. "It couldn't be lost, you know, just mislaid. I'll ask my husband when he comes in if he's seen it."

Ruth licked her lips. "I think I'll get the locks changed all the same," she murmured. "I've been rather nervous since—since it all happened. You see, I know that *I* didn't kill Jonathan Ross, but somebody did. I don't think they like me very much," she added with a light laugh. "And now you say Miss Moir's paintings are valuable—"

"But they're yours. She left them all to you."

Never had Ruth felt farther away from London and the security of law and order. Obviously nobody on Lindisfarne ever gave the idea of theft or murder a passing thought. No wonder the police had been so languid in the face of her urgent summons. They also thought it enough to point out that Miss Moir's paintings belonged to her. Was she being cynical to imagine the insurance company might not see things quite that way?

The insurance company? *What* insurance company? She had taken out insurance on the cottage, but the paintings were something else. She hadn't even mentioned them to the company's assessor. She felt quite faint at the thought.

"Look, don't worry about it," Ruth said to the insulted woman. "If I do change the locks, I'll bring you over a new key sometime. When I go back to London, it'll be nice to know someone's keeping an eye on the place."

"Oh, I'll always do that for you. We get such winds here, you never know when you'll be needing a new tile on the roof, or a new piece of glass in the window. It's no trouble to me to do that for you. What else are neighbours for?''

Ruth laughed. "I always remembered Lindisfarne as being a special place," she said. "I hope it never changes."

"You belong here, that's why you think that."

"I didn't think I really belonged anywhere—well, more London than anywhere else—"

"You were born on Lindisfarne. You'll always be one of us," Mrs. Jenkins insisted.

A nice sentiment, Ruth thought, oddly comforting. The cottage was beginning to seem like home to her, more of a home than she'd ever had. And her neighbours were friendly.

"Would you recognize any of Miss Moir's relatives?" Ruth asked.

"I doubt it, dear." Mrs. Jenkins put a hand on Ruth's arm to make sure she had her full attention. "It isn't for me to be telling you what to do, my dear, but I must tell you that Miss Moir wouldn't have liked for you to invite any of them here. She never told me why she had quarrelled with her family, but you may be sure she had her reasons. She wasn't one to make a great deal out of nothing, not in all the years I knew her. She both liked and trusted her 'Miss Gaynor,' as she called you. It wouldn't do to let her down, would it?"

Ruth dropped a light kiss on the older woman's sweet-smelling cheek. "I'll try not to let her down," she promised. "Let's say I'm beginning to dislike her relations every bit as much as she did. What's more, I think they know Miss Moir left her cottage to me and they don't approve."

Mrs. Jenkins nodded her head sagely. "That nice young man of yours will look after you," she said.

Ruth opened her eyes very wide. "What do you know about him?" she demanded.

"He's staying upstairs in my spare room, that's what I know. No funny business about him. I like him."

Ruth hesitated for only a moment. "So do I," she said.

Aidan hadn't expected his friend, still such a young man, to be in charge of the art brokerage. He unwrapped the Melissa Moir watercolour he had borrowed and laid it on the desk.

"Good God!" Anthony Diamond allowed a broad grin to crease his face. He certainly hadn't anticipated this when he had invited Aidan Wakefield into his office. A few reminiscences, a gentle reproach that as an old friend, Aidan should feel free to waste Anthony's time showing him some amateur painting probably done by his latest girlfriend, and then the quick brush-off—that was what he had been expecting, and he had only gone along with that because he had always liked Aidan, and besides, they had played rugby football together. That wasn't a bond that could be lightly broken. But this! He could hug himself with glee. A Melissa Moir. A genuine Melissa Moir! And just when the whole art world had despaired of the lost paintings ever being seen again.

"Have you any idea what you've got hold of here?"

Aidan watched him with folded arms, his face betraying nothing of the triumph he felt. "Like that, is it?" he drawled.

"I'll say. During her lifetime, the old girl only sold her work when it was absolutely necessary. Then, after she died and the news finally got out—which wasn't for ages because she left instructions no one was to be told so that her family wouldn't harass her heir until everything had been sorted out—all her paintings leapt in value. There aren't many watercolourists whose work can fetch anything like the same figure at auction. The Tate has a couple of Moirs and is known to want to add more to its collection, but there are none at all in any of the galleries in the North. What I'd give to have the handling of even one Moir! It isn't yours, I don't suppose?''

Aidan became more watchful than ever. "If it were mine, how much could I expect for it?''

Tony Diamond considered for a moment, his face flushing with excitement at the mere thought of handling such a sale.

"I would expect at least a six-figure sum—more for a set. If the Getty Foundation heard about it, it could well be more. I'd be sorry to see it go to America, however.''

"Where would you recommend I take it? Sotheby's?''

Mr. Diamond ran suddenly sweaty hands down his trousers. "I'd willingly handle it for you—for less than my usual commission. That is if you can prove ownership and all that sort of thing. Hey, I don't suppose you're the missing heir, are you?''

Aidan began wrapping up the picture again. "It doesn't seem very safe to talk too much about ownership—''

"In case the family succeeds in upsetting the old lady's will?''

Aidan's eyes glinted dangerously. "Melissa Moir treated them pretty shabbily, whichever way you look at it. Families ought to stick together in success as well as in disaster.''

Tony Diamond shook his head. "That's a two-way street in my book. What did they ever do for her?''

Aidan shrugged. "All I know about her is that she was somewhat strange. She could have quarrelled with them about anything. Eccentric old ladies don't have to have a reason for turning on the nearest and dearest and making a misery of their lives, they just do it.''

"Not Melissa Moir!'' Tony maintained stubbornly.

"Knew her, did you?''

The art dealer resented the sneer in the other man's voice. He had always rather liked Aidan Wakefield, but he didn't care for his attitude in this instance.

"Few did!" he said aloud. "I suppose you, with your legal backing, wouldn't be going to help them upset the will?"

Aidan looked suitably vague. "I don't think I know any of the Moir relations—not yet."

"How are you going to recognize them?" Tony grunted. "Do you think they may be leery of coming forward?"

"It could be. You'd know more about that than I."

Aidan's eyes narrowed. "Would I? Why?"

"Weren't you going to defend Ruth Gaynor if Jonathan Ross's murder had come to trial?"

"So?"

"So Jonathan Ross was connected to Melissa Moir by marriage."

"Was he now?" said Aidan.

Chapter Six

"Wake up, sleepyhead."

Ruth groaned and turned over, pulling the blankets up over her head. "I'm not speaking to you," she said.

There was a moment's silence, then Aidan asked tentatively, "Had a bad night?"

"Thanks to you."

He sat down on the edge of her bed. "That sounds promising. What happened? Did you dream of me?"

"If I had, it would have been a nightmare. Who said you could remove my property from my house?"

"I left a note."

"Which I didn't find until after I'd sent for the police. Have you any idea of the value of that painting?"

"Have you?" He sounded cautious.

"I have now. The tides were wrong for the police to come at once." Ruth sat up, pulling the sheet up to her shoulders with a modesty that delighted him. Part of him wished to see much more of her, but another part knew a quiet pleasure that she wasn't going to be rushed into anything. If she ever made a commitment to a man, she would mean every word of it. Aidan hoped it would be him. "I felt foolish enough as it was, first telling them to come running, and then telling them not to bother. It's lucky you weren't here, let me tell you. I was furious!"

She looked pale and tired, as she continued, "And Mrs. Jenkins has mislaid her key to the cottage. She assures me it isn't lost, but anyone could have taken it—"

"*My* Mrs. Jenkins?"

Ruth sniffed. "If you care to think of her that way."

She knew she was asking for trouble, had been ever since she had opened her eyes, but she didn't care. She was conscious of a tingling sensation in her middle. Aidan was so close to her she only had to put out a hand to touch him— not that she would. She might want to, but she knew it wouldn't stop there, and she wasn't ready for anything else. Her head thrown back to stretch her neck, she looked down her nose at him. She had waited thirty years, she thought. She could wait a bit longer until she was absolutely sure that it was what they both wanted, with no secrets between them to knock them off balance in the future.

"I don't like the sound of that," Aidan said slowly.

Ruth fluttered her lashes in what she hoped was a seductive way. "You're very hard to please," she mocked.

"I mean," he said, "I don't like the sound of the key going missing. We'd better get the locks changed."

"We?"

"I'll see to it. I want to make sure you have a proper dead bolt that can't be opened by someone with a plastic card. People up here don't expect to be broken into, but it happens—even on Lindisfarne, it happens."

Ruth examined her fingernails. "The insurance company is in a state of shock," she said at last.

Aidan cast her a quick look of silent enquiry. "You told them about the lost key?"

"Uh-huh. Among other things. Why did you take that painting away, Aidan?"

"I wanted to know a bit more about Melissa Moir."

"Couldn't you have told me that?"

"I thought you might be happier not knowing. What happened to make you guess the truth?"

"You remember I told you that Mrs. Jenkins said Miss Moir had more money than sense. I'd been picturing her as a penniless old recluse, selling her daubs to the tourists in the summer. How wrong can one be?"

"You found out how famous she was?"

Ruth laughed shortly. "To quote Mrs. Jenkins: 'Miss Moir was Miss Moir, it is her paintings that are famous.'"

"Is that how you found out?"

Ruth nodded. "How did you find out?"

"I took the painting to a dealer I know and he told me. You're sitting on a fortune in this cottage, sweetheart."

"Much good it's doing me. I can't afford the insurance premiums, not even the temporary cover they offered me over the phone. I took all the paintings to Berwick and put them in a strongbox at the bank. I spent the afternoon zig-zagging all over the county in case anyone had followed me. I really think I'm going off my head."

Aidan didn't answer for a while. He was too busy laughing at Ruth's description of her antics. Finally, he said, "Atta girl. I'll go downstairs and make some coffee. Feel like breakfast?"

"Not really."

"How about taking a picnic with us to Berwick?"

She shot a petulant look at him. "I don't want to go to Berwick again."

"You haven't any choice. We won't find solid locks anywhere nearer than Berwick."

She lay back against the pillows. "You go," she urged. "I want to stay here."

Aidan looked as stubborn as she felt. "I'm not leaving you on your own," he growled. "You'll feel better after you have a cup of coffee."

She certainly hoped so. "Why should you care about me?" she demanded. "You may amuse yourself by worrying about me now, but what about when you go back to London, your holiday over? I'll still be on my own then, won't I?"

"We'll talk about it," he said.

"When?"

"In Berwick," Aidan snapped, thinking he'd better get Ruth her coffee—and quick.

Aidan was gone down the stairs before Ruth could think of anything else to say to delay him. She shut her eyes, not liking herself very much. What did she want from him anyway? She didn't even know if she could trust him, or if he was on the other side, sent by Miss Moir's family to steal her inheritance. If she couldn't trust Aidan Wakefield, she didn't want to know. What was the old tag? Wasn't it: *Better to have loved and lost than never to have loved at all*?

Ruth lay completely still, her whole being concentrated on the terrifying reality of where her thoughts were leading her.

Love is sweet, but tastes best with bread. The proverb came into her mind from nowhere. Breakfast was what she needed to restore herself to normality, she thought. She was afraid of love, afraid of the heartbreak she was sure it would bring her. *Love is sweet?* Her daily bread had never come mixed with love, not since she had left Miss Moir, but she could imagine it added a whole dimension to living that people like Aidan took for granted. The trouble was that she hadn't much confidence in her ability to love, or to be loved. She couldn't imagine what it was like, mixing loving and living as naturally as someone mixed the flour with the water to make bread. Could she learn to love as she learned a part for the theatre—as most people learned it from their parents? She didn't know.

Aidan had brought some croissants in with him, hot, buttery crescents of pastry that she never would have allowed herself on her own, for she was always careful of what she ate, solemnly counting the calories in case she started to put on weight.

"I don't know how you keep so fit when I see the food you choose to eat," she muttered crossly. She didn't want him to know that walking into the kitchen and seeing him there, as if he *belonged* there, had sent her whole body into a tizzy of excitement, as if she were a thirsty man finding water in a desert.

"I'm on holiday. Remember?"

"Over-indulgence is bad for one," Ruth chided, but received only a broad grin as a response.

Aidan poured a mug of coffee and put it down in front of her. "You know," he remarked, "until I knew you, I never realized how important it was to spoil children and make them feel a bit special from time to time. Never mind, working on the principle that it's never too late, I plan to spoil you rotten all day—"

"At my age?" Ruth felt it quite safe to laugh at him from behind her mug of coffee.

"You didn't allow me to finish," he went on with offended dignity. "I'll spoil you by day, and make love to you all night. How's that for a programme?"

She choked over her coffee. "Indeed you won't!"

He buttered a croissant and held it out, touching her lips with it, until she could resist no longer and took a bite out of it. His eyes crinkled at the corners in amusement at her outraged face. "How you manage to persuade a paying audience that you're familiar with the feelings you portray on stage is beyond me."

"I'm an excellent actress," she averred.

He brushed a crumb from the corner of her mouth with a gentle finger. "You don't fool me, Ruth Gaynor. Underneath, you're a vulnerable young girl, afraid of your own shadow. I doubt you even realize how beautiful you are."

"Oh yes, I do. I put on my beauty every morning in front of the looking glass and take it off again at night."

He shook his head at her. "It shines out of your eyes and appears in a fleeting expression. Sometimes, you're so lovely, it takes my breath away."

She didn't know what to say to that. The compliment didn't have to be true to please her, and there were a thousand graceful responses she might have made. But she knew, and he would know, that they would be couched in other people's words and not her own, and were therefore worthless at that particular moment. She took a deep breath, steadying herself, and made the mistake of looking straight at him. His dark eyes gave no hint of what he was thinking—and then, as suddenly, he smiled at her, taking her breath away as he had said she sometimes did his.

"Don't," she said at last, deliberately breaking up the moment. "I don't like playing games."

His eyebrows rose as if it to mock her. She knew she had hurt him and wished the words unsaid.

Her eyes dropped and the colour edged up into her face. "I'm sorry. I didn't mean that."

He smiled again. "Am I getting to you at last?"

"Yes, damn you."

"And you resent it? I wonder why?"

"Because it can't lead anywhere. Once we're both back at work—"

"Ah. I thought we'd come back to your work sooner or later. As cover, my darling, it's getting thinner and thinner, especially since you don't appear to have much work at the moment. Who's playing games now, I ask you?"

That did it. He'd roused her anger as nothing else could have done. Her whole being burned with indignation, revelling in its protective armour. Ruth's eyes flashed. "You know very well why I'm not working. But as soon as Judith finds me something to do—"

"Yes, yes, but what has that to do with me?" he demanded.

Stunned, she could only stare at him. What had it to do with him? If her work was almost exclusively in London, so was his. If she occasionally travelled to Birmingham, or even as far north as Manchester, so did he. There was nowhere she could go without his being able to turn up as easily as if they worked in next-door offices. "I knew you wouldn't understand." She sighed. "I put everything I have into my work. I don't have anything left over for anything else."

"You remind me of Elizabeth Browning. You remember her *Sonnets from the Portuguese*?"

Still furious, Ruth didn't want to admit that she did. "Why did she call herself that?" she asked, forcing a cool tone of voice.

"Because her husband thought she looked Portuguese. How did it go? For frequent tears have run the colours from my life, and left so dead and pale a stuff—"

"I *never* cry," Ruth insisted. Then she hesitated, seeing the doubtful expression on his face. She remembered the poem—she knew it by heart. If he could quote from it, so could she. "—it were not fitly done to give the same as pillow to thy head. Go farther! let it serve to trample on."

"She didn't show much confidence in herself, either, did she?" he said.

He sounded as if he knew exactly how *both* women felt. Ruth could feel her inner motivations being dragged out of her as a dentist draws out teeth. And the sensation was equally unpleasant. "I'm not surprised," she said. "Look at her father. He wasn't exactly a bundle of laughs. Didn't he disinherit every child of his who married in his lifetime?"

"Mad as a hatter," Aidan agreed. "But Robert Browning wasn't mad. A bit romantic, perhaps, but not mad. Once he'd stilled her doubts, they made a very happy couple." He came towards her, dropping a quick kiss on her cheek. "I kiss your cheek, catch your soul's warmth—I pluck the rose and love it more than tongue can speak—then the good minute goes."

One thing about being an actress was that one couldn't help but have a good memory—but barristers? She had never met anyone outside the profession who could quote poetry at will, let alone both Robert *and* Elizabeth Browning! "The minute goes. That's the point," she said bitingly.

"Is it? Where there's love, the minute can always be renewed. That's what Robert proved to Elizabeth, and what I, my darling, mean to prove to you."

Ruth cast him a mocking glance, but she was shaken by the promise that lay behind the words, more shaken than she wanted to acknowledge to herself—and much more than she wanted him to know.

"Is that why we're going on a picnic?" she asked demurely.

He looked amused also. "So that I can seduce you? I'd stay at home for that. Making love in the great outdoors sounds all very well, but I think it may rain."

"Very likely," she agreed. It had rained practically every day that summer. "But we are going for a picnic?"

"Certainly, we are. But we'll go in my car this time—and I'll drive."

Ruth saw the reason for his choice when she had packed up the picnic and went out to find him. Aidan had no difficulty folding his frame behind the driving wheel of the German car. A slight smile on his lips, he placed the picnic basket between them, helped her fasten her belt, bidding her operate either the radio or the cassette player.

"You must be doing much better than I thought if you can afford a car like this!" she said.

"Well enough. I'm lucky to be in good chambers—"

"Your father's influence?"

"My grandfather's, and the head of chambers where I was before. But nobody can win your cases for you in court. You're on your own there, pitted against some of the best brains in England."

"And that's why you like it?"

"I like to win," he admitted.

She already knew that. More than that, she felt a bond between them because she imagined that appearing in court wasn't so very different from making an appearance on the stage. He probably used the same tricks of the trade to win and hold the jury as she used to get the audience pulling for her. They were both a couple of old hams Ruth smiled to herself, pleased by the idea.

The causeway was only just clear of the tide when they crossed it. People were already waiting to drive in the opposite direction, though, nervously getting in and out of their cars as they tried to make up their minds whether it was safe to go. The people in the front two cars were obviously travelling together. The man in the lead eyed the causeway and looked back at his companion. He made the thumbs-up signal and set off, the woman behind him following more slowly.

"Funny," said Ruth. "I could swear that woman was Sylvia Ross."

Aidan frowned. "Jonathan Ross's widow?"

Ruth cast him a quick look. He didn't sound particularly surprised. "Do you know her?" she asked.

"I know of her. More to the point, how well do *you* know her?"

"I've seen her around."

Ruth didn't want to say more than that. She was beginning to wonder all over again exactly what he was doing, sitting next to her, going for a picnic with her, just as if they had met under the most propitious circumstances in the world. Could she trust him?

"Did you know she's related to your Miss Moir?" he asked in the same conversational tone he always used when discussing the Ross murder.

"Sylvia Ross?" The shock of it made her feel hot and cold all over. "How do you know that?"

"I just wondered if you did."

"I don't know any of Miss Moir's relations," Ruth protested.

"Okay, I believe you. I'm glad the police don't seem to have made the connection, however. It would have told against you in court."

She felt a renewed wave of shock pass through her. "You mean that could have been why I killed him? Because of Miss Moir's will?"

"It would have made a better motive than the one they had," he said dryly.

Ruth could only stare at him. "I still don't understand," she managed to say at last. "Why should anyone go to such lengths to gain a cottage? It's a beautiful place, and I love it, but someone like Sylvia Ross could live anywhere she chose—and not in a tiny cottage, either!''

"The cottage is neither here nor there," he answered. "I think it's the paintings they want to get their hands on!"

"They only have to ask for them—"

He reached out a hand, taking hers comfortably in his. She swallowed her apprehension that he should think it all right to drive along with only one hand on the wheel. The car probably had power steering, and goodness knows what else. "Was Miss Moir's will ever read out to you?" he asked.

She shook her head.

"Well, that's the next thing we've got to do—get our hands on the will."

"I don't suppose the rest of the will applied to me," she objected. "It would feel like reading someone else's correspondence."

"Rubbish. Wills are made to be looked at. I'll bet her relatives didn't hesitate to provide themselves with a copy of it."

"That's different. They're family."

"And they knew what a Melissa Moir painting was worth."

Ruth chewed on her lower lip. "Did you?" she asked at last. "Is that why you took the painting to Durham with you?"

"I couldn't see anything else of particular value in the cottage," he answered. "They had to be after something. You don't go to the lengths of killing someone if there's no pot of gold at the end of the rainbow."

She digested that in silence. "I'm afraid!" Ruth found herself confessing. But she didn't want to give up Miss Moir's paintings. "Let's not go to Berwick. Let's go back to the cottage and see what Sylvia wants."

"I doubt she means to call on you openly. If she does, Mrs. Jenkins will see to her. Forget the whole thing, my love, and concentrate on me instead."

"And what is that going to do for me?" Ruth asked suspiciously.

"You must be getting old if you have to ask me that!" Aidan retorted, his eyes gleaming with satisfaction as the colour slid up into her face. "What I'd like to do is kiss it better, and keep you safe by my side forever more. I've half a mind to do that, anyway."

"I might have something to say about that."

He groaned aloud. "Like what?"

"Well, there's my work—"

"I'm not talking about your working hours, *hinny*."

But those were the only hours Ruth knew about. She retreated into herself, not expecting to win the argument and not trusting that he was as uninterested in Sylvia Ross's turning up at Lindisfarne as he said he was. He, too, could have been related to Miss Moir. In fact, given the choice, she would have thought him a more likely suspect than Sylvia Ross. She tried to recall what she could remember of Sylvia and came up with only what she'd heard: a blowsy woman, a shadow who had followed in Jonathan's wake, trying, never successfully, to advance her own acting career.

What else did Ruth know about her? That she smiled with her teeth and not with her eyes, and that was all. It wasn't a great deal, really, but then she hadn't known much about Jonathan Ross, either. She must have heard his name a million times, who hadn't? Ruth hadn't liked what she knew about Jonathan Ross, but she had known it would have been quite a boost to her career to work for him and so she hadn't hesitated to meet with him. What had she had to lose?

Judith hadn't liked it, though. But then Judith was the only person who cared about Ruth as a person and, being her agent and one of the best, she had always tried to steer Ruth's career into paths where she would stay in control of her own roles and her own future.

"I've seen too many talented people mess up their careers by getting involved with these characters who only use them to further their own grip on the theatre," Judith has said to Ruth.

Judith could be as ruthless as anyone, Ruth had sometimes thought, but she had guarded Ruth as carefully as if she had been her sister, only allowing her to take parts that did something for her, even if they paid less. They had, both of them, just begun to reap the rewards when Ruth had found herself accused of murder. Would she ever get a decent part again?

Aidan and Ruth reached the turnoff to Berwick almost before she knew it.

"Berwick ought to be in Scotland," he observed. "Their football team plays in the Scottish League."

"And the old county of Berwick is in Scotland," Ruth added. "I think the city must have a split personality. They've changed sides across the border so often, they must be dizzy with it all. Have you been here before?"

"I've passed through once or twice."

Ruth became quite excited at the thought of showing off *her* city to him. "We'll have our picnic on the ramparts," she decided. "They're unique and well worth visiting. You see, when the first Queen Elizabeth came to the throne, there were a lot of people in these parts who would have preferred her Catholic cousin, Mary, Queen of Scots, in her place. Elizabeth was really in mortal danger all those early years and poor Mary was an awful fool. Well, Berwick was English at the time, so Elizabeth hired an Italian to fortify the city, fearing the Scots would come pouring over the border with the help of the French, who had their own interest in Mary, having married her off to the heir to their throne and brought her up in France. The result was that the poor girl despised her own people, the Scots, whirling about in their kilts and assaulting her ears with the bagpipes. She threw away her popularity, making enemies of old friends. Her cousin, Elizabeth, never made that mistake. Having survived her father's revenge on her mother, her brother's reign and then her sister's, Elizabeth was a survivor before she was anything else.''

Aidan heard the note of admiration in Ruth's voice and knew he was listening to another survivor who knew what it was like to make her own way against the odds. He wondered if that was what Miss Moir had seen in Ruth. It would explain why she had trusted her with the paintings she had wanted to deny her greedy family. Even now, he didn't think Ruth fully realized she was sitting on a fortune.

The sun was shining as Ruth and Aidan made their way up onto the high bastions of Berwick, although the first of the rain was already threatening in the gusts of wind that caught at their clothes and hair. It was no surprise that they had the stone parapets to themselves.

"Not really picnic weather, is it?" Aidan remarked.

"If you live up here, you get so that you ignore the weather. You'd never do anything otherwise," Ruth replied sagely.

"I don't remember it raining every day in Durham. Looking back, I remember some pretty good summers on the whole." He came to a halt, taking in the view below them of the Tweed. The bridge that joined the city to the rest of England was magnificent in its proportions. Looking for food, the flocks of birds came and went over the estuary.

Ruth put her arm through his. "How do you like my old hometown?" she asked him.

"It'll do," he said to conceal his wonderment. "It isn't Durham, but it'll do."

Ruth was proud of the picnic she'd put together. She had used the remains of the curry they had made together, to make a curry puff. Cold, it didn't taste half as spicy as it had when they first had it. The pastry was so light it crumbled even as they ate. Pastry was one of the few things Ruth had always been able to make, even as a child.

"If I could be sure I'll work again, I'd be really happy right now," Ruth said. "I must give Judith a ring and find out if she has anything for me."

"Won't she ring you?"

"She's busy. One never realizes how the days are slipping by when one's busy. I need the work."

"Running short of cash?" he asked her, dropping the words like bait in front of her nose.

"I surely am. Even subletting my apartment in London hasn't helped all that much. I'll ask Judith to try and get me a few advertisements until something else turns up. I'm so far away up here, but I didn't dare stay on in London and eat up my savings."

"You didn't think of selling something to keep you going?"

She laughed. "What would I sell? I doubt the Salvation Army would think it worth their while to carry away my furniture if I gave it to them!"

"You could sell one of the Melissa Moir paintings. That would keep you for a while."

She turned a shocked, ashen face towards him. "Sell something of Miss Moir's? What a horrible idea. If she left them to me, along with the house, she must have had a good reason, and I'm quite sure it wasn't so that I should sell them and live off the proceeds. That's what her family would have liked to do.'' She was silent for a long moment, then came to a decision. "Perhaps it would be a good idea for me to read her will sometime.''

"Oh, yes. As I mentioned this morning, one's will is public property after it's been proved.''

Ruth was busy with her own thoughts. "I'd go back to her solicitor if he were still alive. Do you think he might have had a partner?''

"Give me his name and I'll find out,'' he offered.

She gave him a long, level look. "Why are you doing all this for me? What are you going to get out of it, Aidan?''

"I hope to get to know you better. Won't you trust me?''

She had learned the hard way never to trust anyone. "I want to. Are you sure you didn't follow me up here because you were between girlfriends and weren't doing anything else particular for your holiday?''

"If that were all, I'd have chosen someone with a less prickly exterior than Miss Ruth Gaynor's!''

"You'd be prickly—'' she began, exasperated.

"If I had beautiful eyes like yours, I'd expect half of England to follow me the length of the nation. The *male* half.''

She laughed. "Don't men have beautiful eyes?''

"I was waiting for you to notice,'' Aidan said, looking hurt.

"You have nice eyes. And gorgeous hands,'' she comforted him. "And,'' she went on, trying to sound stern through her laughter, "all the talk in the world about my beauty won't get you anywhere with me. I know exactly what my plusses and minuses are, kind sir, and I know I'm not beautiful at all.''

He put his hands on her shoulders, claiming her complete attention. "Sometimes you're as plain as any woman I've seen. I thought that when I first saw you. And then the beauty comes shining through, when you move your head, or lift an eyebrow, or maybe smile at me. If you were a classic beauty I probably would have forgotten all about you by now. As it is, I hate to miss a moment of your company because I never know what to expect. I've just got used to one aspect of you, then you change. It's like receiving an electric charge from time to time. One can get addicted to things like that."

His fingers were bruising the flesh of her shoulders, but she barely noticed. She licked her dry lips and knew even as she did so he would take it as an invitation. He did. He lowered his mouth to hers in a kiss so passionate and forceful that everything else went out of her mind and she was conscious only of him and the effect he was having on her.

The rain started with the suddenness of someone turning on a tap. Aidan brushed her damp face with his fingers.

"I don't have much luck kissing you, do I?" he murmured.

She leaned her forehead against his shoulder. "Don't let a little thing like rain stop you. I'm getting to like it," Ruth said, surprising herself.

He smiled. "That sounds promising. I think we'd better go back to the car, however, before we're both soaked."

"All right."

"Some people enjoy kissing in cars," he said hopefully.

Ruth shook her head. The rain had come just in time. "We're both too old for that," she said firmly.

He began to run, pulling her after him and laughing over his shoulder. "You've never tried it. That's all that's the matter with you," he affirmed.

Sadly, it was true, but there was no reason to admit it. Thirty was far too old to start behaving like a teenager, and she wasn't going to try it. Not if she could help it, she added, crossing the fingers of her free hand. He probably wouldn't ask her to, anyway.

As they carefully drove through the downpour, away from the stone walls of Berwick, Ruth realized that Aidan had respected her firm request, and that she was strangely disappointed.

Chapter Seven

Ruth didn't know what she had expected. She had imagined Sylvia to be the possessor of the missing key, to have broken into the cottage and to have removed everything she could have laid her hands on, except Melissa Moir's watercolours, now safely tucked away in the vault. It came as a shock when nothing seemed to have been tampered with at all. Seeing Mrs. Jenkins across the road, she called out to her, "Has anyone been asking for me?"

Mrs. Jenkins was eager to stop and gossip. "My dear, your house key was on its hook all the time. I can't understand how I came to think it was missing. I asked my husband if he'd seen it anywhere when he came in for his lunch—and there it was, as large as life. I felt a right fool, let me tell you."

"It wasn't there when we looked before," Ruth said firmly, feeling suddenly afraid. "I was there."

"Well, I can't explain it, but it's back on its nail now, safe and sound. Thought I'd tell you, in case you needed it for anything. I do hate it when things go missing, don't you?"

With real feeling, Ruth agreed that she did. "Aidan took me into Berwick to get some new locks. He's busy putting them on the doors now. I was going to come over with a key for you later, but I may as well give it to you now."

Mrs. Jenkins's startled look made Ruth wonder if anyone ever changed locks on Lindisfarne, let alone for such a paltry reason as a missing key.

"He's a lawyer," she found herself explaining. "He's worried about the insurance. Men!" she added in conspiratorial tones.

"Aye, they're all the same. Mr. Jenkins was in a great way about that key when he heard it was missing. Ever so angry that I'd forgotten to tell him before. Seems he's seen someone hanging around where they shouldn't be. That really upset him."

"Oh? When was this?"

"Goodness knows, love. I asked him why he didn't tell me before and he said he hadn't wanted to worry me, but now if keys are going missing... Isn't that just like a man? They expect you to read their minds."

Ruth agreed, then said goodbye to Mrs. Jenkins and rushed off home. As she got closer to the cottage, she thought she heard a telephone ringing.

Aidan was standing behind the door when she went inside. He reached out an arm, fielding her neatly as she tripped over the bag of tools he had borrowed from somewhere to put on the new locks.

"Where are you dashing to?" he asked her.

"I thought I heard the telephone."

"You did."

"Was it Judith?"

His hand was still on her waist. Ruth tried to escape by wiggling away from him. It didn't work. A smile spread across his features as he dropped a kiss on her open mouth. "Don't you know anyone else?" Aidan asked.

Ruth made a valiant attempt to catch her breath. "I need the work," she wailed.

"I need you," he whispered.

She thought her knees were going to give way under her. She hooked an arm about his neck and kissed him back. He tasted good and she helped herself to some more of the same with an increasing urgency. Her tongue tangled with his and she tore herself out of his arms, frightened by the depth of the emotions that threatened to overwhelm him.

"What's wrong?" he groaned.

Ruth stared at him as if she were St. George confronting the dragon. "I've—I've never experienced *that* before!"

"Is that all?" he said.

"All!" She sat down hard on the nearest chair. She was at a loss for words. "I'm going to ring Judith," she declared.

His eyes narrowed, taking in her flushed face and the quick rise and fall of her breasts. "Thirty years old," he taunted her.

"I suppose you were at it when you were about fourteen!" she retorted.

"It's as well that one of us knows what he's doing, don't you think?" Aidan said seriously.

Her eyes widened. "How do you make that out?"

"Loving's like everything else; it gets better with practice."

Ruth looked away, the colour staining her cheeks. "I prefer not to discuss it," she averred sharply. "Not that there's anything to discuss, but, well, you know what I mean!"

"I haven't the faintest idea. I don't think you have either. And don't think that demure expression is going to stop me from kissing you again, my darling. I'm going to court you from now until doomsday if that's what it takes—"

"*Court* me? D-don't be ridiculous!"

He put his hands on his hips, looking larger than life and completely immovable. "It's a nice, old-fashioned word for a nice, old-fashioned way of talking a girl into loving a man."

There didn't seem to be anything Ruth could say to that. She sniffed angrily, sure that he had had the better of the argument but unable to see quite how it had come about. "I'm going to ring Judith," she said again.

"I should if I were you. She has some advertisements for you—"

"Why didn't you say so before?" Ruth demanded.

"Something distracted me."

Suddenly, Ruth felt like a heel. "I hope you understand that I don't have affairs. I'm sorry."

He smiled, and everything seemed back to normal again. "Don't be! I've given them up myself. You get a life sentence for what I have in mind."

"You mean, you'd like to wring my neck?" She smiled back at him.

"Something like that," he said, but Ruth saw the warmth fading from his eyes.

It took a while to get through to Judith's London office. Ruth dialed the number until her finger was sore, making slanderous statements about the telephone company as she did so. When she finally heard the ringing sound at the other end of the line, she breathed a sigh of relief.

"Judith?" she asked as soon as the phone was answered.

"Who else?" The laconic response restored Ruth's equilibrium as nothing else could have done. "Did that gorgeous hunk of manhood tell you I have some work for you?''

"How do you know he's gorgeous?"

Judith chuckled. "He's up there with you, isn't he?"

"Not exactly," Ruth said primly. "He's staying with Mrs. Jenkins, my neighbour."

"That's *your* story. Look, I'll hurry up because you're paying for this call. I have three advertisements for you—beauty products, guaranteeing no cruelty to man or beast in their production. Interested?"

"I'll say!"

"Good. How soon can you be in London?"

"Tomorrow. I haven't anywhere to live in London right now, though. How long is this going to take?"

"Be my guest," Judith invited her. "That is, unless you prefer to stay with the man in your life? I'll quite understand—"

"I keep telling you, we're not on those terms," Ruth insisted.

Judith only laughed. "Oh well, here's hoping," she said. "I'll expect to hear all about it when I see you tomorrow."

"Thanks," said Ruth. "I mean that, Judith. I can really do with the work."

"I know. These ought to do you a bit of good. They're funny and sympathetic. I have hopes they'll lead to better things. I'll tell you all when I see you."

"Yes. Thanks again," Ruth said excitedly.

"Think nothing of it. That's what I'm here for."

Ruth's face shone as she put down the phone and turned to Aidan. "Work at last," she exclaimed.

"I know, I heard. I'll drive you down to London tomorrow."

She sat up very straight. "I think I ought to go in my own car," she began solemnly.

"I'll drive you, *hinny*, or you won't go."

She blinked. "Is that an order?" she asked, preparing to do battle for her independence, especially when it came to her work.

"It's a long drive and my car's bigger than yours. I feel like a sardine at his last gasp in yours, so I suggest we go in mine."

"Do you want to go to London tomorrow?" she asked him, agreeing with his reasoning. "I thought you came up here on holiday?"

"For you, lady, anything."

Sitting on the edge of her bed, Ruth set the alarm for an early hour. She felt like crying inside at the thought of leaving behind her home and these few idyllic days with Aidan. At least there were some good, solid locks on the doors, she thought, and Mrs. Jenkins and her husband watching out for strangers. She was leaving her house in good hands. She was glad to know Miss Moir's paintings were all safely stowed away in the vaults of the Royal Bank of Scotland. And tomorrow, she would have Aidan by her side nearly all day. Ruth fell asleep wondering if he would kiss her again or whether he would bring his "courtship" to an end as soon as he was back in the familiar surroundings of his everyday life. She would miss him when he did give up and leave her to her own devices.

The crash on the door startled her into wakefulness. The whole house had shuddered under the force of the blow. Ruth sat up in bed, clutching the bedclothes to her. She thought she heard the rasp of a key that refused to budge and thanked God silently that Aidan had changed the locks. Reluctantly, she struggled out of bed. Forcing her warm feet into cold slippers, she hurried down the stairs.

Aidan's locks worked smoothly and without a sound, quite unlike the rusty ones they had replaced that had always been a struggle to force open and shut. He had put a chain on the door as well. Ruth put it on and opened the door a crack.

"Who's there?" she asked, trembling.

There was no answer.

She thought she could hear heavy breathing. Prickles of fear were travelling up and down her spine before she realized that all she could hear was herself.

But those earlier sounds hadn't been in her imagination or in her dreams. She wished Aidan were with her now, and castigated herself as a coward and a fool. What could Aidan do to help her?

Locking the door again with enormous care, Ruth considered whether to leave the chain on. She decided the new locks ought to be sufficient to keep out all intruders, whereas the chain would only prevent Aidan from coming in the next morning. She was still worrying about it as she went into the kitchen and made herself a cup of tea. What a time to be worrying about Aidan's hurt feelings, when she was in fear for her life.

Ruth sat in a daze in the kitchen, drinking her tea and trying to work up her courage sufficiently to go back to bed, when another knock came at the door, followed by the sound of the door opening. The chain held and she could hear Aidan swearing under his breath. Full of righteous indignation, she stalked down the hall to let him in.

"Just what do you think you're doing at this time of night?" she demanded.

"I was about to ask you the same thing. I saw your light on and wondered what was up."

She sank back on the wooden chair, making a gesture towards the teapot. "Help yourself. Aidan, there was this crashing noise. I know someone was trying to get in. But why?''

"After the paintings, I daresay," he murmured.

She gave him a wide-eyed look of indignation. "Miss Moir's paintings?"

"My dear, you're going to have to face up to the fact that they're worth a mint of money—''

"I know that. I'm still reeling with shock at what the insurance is going to cost. I wonder if she thought of that when she left them, unprotected, in a cottage that is constantly damp and seldom inhabited?''

"I reckon she thought you'd do something about all that," Aidan suggested.

"She didn't know the first thing about me.''

"Perhaps not. She seems to have liked what she did know of you a great deal better than she did her family.''

Ruth took a deep breath. "Why me?" She sighed. "It's such a ghastly responsibility. Thank God all the paintings are safely stowed away in the bank. They can't stay there forever, however, and then what am I going to do?''

"You haven't considered selling?"

"*Selling?* But that would be a terrible thing to do. That's what her family would have done with them.''

"She might have wanted you to have the money," Aidan pointed out.

Ruth's look was contemptuous. "Of course she didn't. She could have sold them all herself. Oh well, I'm going back to bed." She cast a nervous look over her shoulder into the shadowed hall. "I wish I knew what was going on. Aidan, promise me you don't have anything to do with it?''

He crossed his heart. "I promise. I don't like to think of you in this house by yourself though. Why don't you go across to Mrs. Jenkins and leave me here to finish the night in your bed?"

She didn't care for the idea. If he wasn't on the level, he could spend the hours before dawn riffling through her things and she would never know. But she didn't want to stay on in the house on her own, either.

"There is a spare bedroom," she said awkwardly.

"So there is." He grinned at her.

She looked down her nose at him. "That's not an invitation to visit me in my room."

"No, ma'am!"

"Well then, what is there to look so smug about?"

"You look warm and cuddly in your night-clothes. I shall look forward to seeing you over the breakfast table—"

"I shall be *dressed* for breakfast!"

"You can't control my imagination though, can you?" he pointed out. "That's all my own."

"Perhaps you'd rather go back to Mrs. Jenkins?" she said pointedly.

"Mmm. I wonder if she smells as sweet and womanly as you do when she rises from her bed." He sniffed the air. "Mmm," he said again. "Maybe it's the bath oil you use."

Ruth clinked her cup against its saucer. "Have you quite finished?" she asked him dangerously.

His grin was far too knowing, almost as if he could read her mind, which was too bad, for she had an over-active imagination, also. "Are you going to help me make up the bed?" There was laughter in his voice.

She supposed that she owed him that much, so she put the tea things in the sink and then preceded him up the stairs. She hoped the spare room bed was less damp than her own had been that first night, before she had bought an electric underblanket. In silence, she found a couple of rubber, hot-water bottles and handed them to him.

"Will I need these?" he asked. He read the answer on her face. "You see what I'm prepared to suffer for your sake?"

"Let's hope you don't fall sick of an ague!"

He laughed. "What is an ague?"

"I haven't the slightest idea!" But she did know. It was a chill of the nether regions. She knew that because somebody had died of it, or had come pretty close to it, in one of Shakespeare's plays.

Ruth turned and buried her hands in the lavender-smelling cupboard, sorting through the ancient sheets. She wanted to find Miss Moir's special linens, so comfortable and neatly preserved. They would impress Aidan. As she handed him the sheets, Ruth realized she'd never taken care of another person in her life, had never acted as a host, certainly. She'd always thought she'd be too nervous to have people over. She didn't feel that way now. But before she let her feelings run away from her, Ruth thought it best to bid Aidan a hasty good-night.

If Ruth had thought she wouldn't be able to shut her eyes again that night, she was quite wrong. She fell back into bed and slept right through until her alarm went off and she was brought, groaning, back to consciousness and the prospect of the long drive south to London.

It was unexpectedly pleasant to have Aidan to share the last chores with her. She left him to lock up as she carried her case out to his car and amused herself by playing with the central locking system, a feature she had never had on any of her cars.

"I'll split the driving with you—if you'll trust me to drive this thing," she offered as he drove off.

"Okay, four hours on, four hours off," he agreed.

On the whole it was easy driving, straight down the A1, across the link road to the M11, and into the city. Easy driving didn't make it any shorter, however. Ruth doubted she could have done the whole distance in one day in her own car. Sitting comfortably in Aidan's, she didn't mind the heavy traffic half so much. Besides, Aidan drove so well that she didn't have to spend the whole journey worrying over whether they would arrive in one piece. On the contrary, she enjoyed travelling beside him, talking sometimes, wandering off into a daydream sometimes, and, at regular intervals, stopping for a break, a cup of coffee and a change of the driver.

"Mind if I call in at my chambers before I take you to Judith's place?" he asked as they came off the M1.

"Of course not."

She was intrigued to see the place where he had his office. The building looked like something out of Dickens, as did the clerk. He handed Aidan a couple of briefs, tied with the pink strings that Aidan explained had come to be known universally as "red tape."

"Anything interesting here?" Aidan asked the clerk.

"I think you may like the second one, Mr. Wakefield. The top one is strictly bread-and-butter—and none the worse for that."

"Indeed."

"And how are you doing, Miss Gaynor?" asked the shrewd clerk.

Ruth blinked, surprised he knew who she was. "Better, thank you," she said demurely. She would have liked to say something more original, something that didn't sound as though she had been suffering from some illness rather than an accusation of murder.

"I hope you'll soon be back at work," the old clerk said. "You're a great favourite of my wife's"

"I am?"

If she was startled, Aidan looked as pleased and as proud as if he were responsible for her whole career. "Miss Gaynor has come to London to star in some advertisements."

"One doesn't 'star' in an advertisement," Ruth objected.

"As far as I'm concerned, you do," he said simply.

"As far as my wife is concerned also," Mr. Trout added.

Ruth wouldn't have dreamed of smiling at his name, which she suspected gave him as much amusement as it did anyone else, but she did wonder that he should be so unsurprised by her being with Aidan. Her case was over, hopefully, and both men knew it. It gave her an odd, fluttery feeling to think that Aidan might have told this man that he was going north to find her.

"Right, I'll take these home with me," Aidan told him, clutching the two briefs in his hand. "Anything else? It's been a long drive down for Miss Gaynor."

"Nothing else, sir. You take Miss Gaynor home safe and I'll see you first thing on Monday morning. There's nothing urgent here."

It was only a short way after that to Judith's flat. Ruth sat for a moment in the car, looking up at the familiar building with its stately curved corners. From where she was sitting, she could see Judith's balcony, laden down with potted plants, and adorned with an orange-eared, white-faced cat peering down at her. "Will I see you again?" she asked at last, turning to Aidan.

"Do you want to?"

"Yes."

The appalling baldness of that single word burned through her mind in a flash. She looked away, searching for some way of softening the embarrassing truth in that monosyllable.

Aidan warmed to the vulnerable expression in Ruth's eyes. "Then try and keep me away," he said gently. "I'll always be there, *hinny*."

"I don't see why," she said, turning her face away from him.

"I told you why. I'm courting you, Ruth Gaynor, in the old-fashioned way. Sooner or later, I'm hoping for an old-fashioned answer from you."

She smiled at him almost shyly. "I'd better go in."

"I'll carry your bag."

She didn't argue with him, though she could have quite well carried it up the stairs by herself. For some reason she couldn't explain to herself, she wanted Judith to see him. It might have been to have a second opinion, as it were, but she didn't think it was that. She knew now that she was falling in love with Aidan Wakefield and, if she felt like that about him, what did it matter if Judith approved or not?

Judith was standing in the doorway of her apartment, the door already open, when they reached her floor. She hugged Ruth as she always did and then held out her hand to Aidan.

"So you weren't wasting your time after all," Judith said to him.

"Far from it."

"I hope you found what you were looking for."

Their eyes glinted with shared laughter. "I'm getting there," Aidan said lazily. "Did I say thank you?"

Ruth looked from one to the other of them. "It was you who gave him my address?" she asked Judith.

"Nothing of the sort," the lady returned calmly. "You know I never give out my clients' addresses. I was tempted to point him in the right direction, but I didn't even do that."

"No, she was maddeningly discreet," Aidan said with a grin.

Ruth wasn't as cross as she might have been. She could believe that Judith hadn't actually written out her address and given it to him, but there had obviously been some exchange between them or they wouldn't be greeting each other as old friends now.

"By the way," said Judith, "someone else has been after your address whom I didn't feel inclined to help. Remember Sylvia Ross?"

Ruth started. "She came to see you?"

"She's looking for a new agent," Judith said dryly. "Come in, both of you. This is something I want you to hear."

Ruth flung herself into one of the comfortable armchairs. "Tell me about Sylvia Ross," she said, trying to appear casual.

Judith gave her a cautious look. "I'm *not* taking her on."

"No," Ruth agreed. "I've always heard she couldn't act her way out of a paper bag."

Judith made an obvious effort to be just. "I don't know about that. She's never had much of a chance with Jon always putting her down. She's trimmed down since I last saw her and looks a great deal better for it—as long as one doesn't get too close. She had some sad story that her marriage to Jon had been on the rocks long before he was killed and that she had hoped to save it by putting a lot of money into his last productions. Something went wrong apparently, and now she's looking for something else."

"I've never seen Sylvia as an 'angel,'" Ruth muttered.

Aidan looked up sharply. "An 'angel?' You mean someone who puts money into a show? Doesn't it take real wealth to do that?"

"If she were doing it alone," Judith answered him. "She may have organized a whole group of backers for him, using his name as bait. She acted very depressed, and she cried almost as much as she talked. Crocodile tears, I thought. I was glad to get rid of her."

"But what did she really want?" Ruth insisted. "Did you get the impression she wanted to make it back on the boards, or was she just fishing for information? I suppose she knows you're my agent?"

"I don't know." Judith made a face. "Yes, I'd say she does know that. She said that if she could get hold of the money she'd like to do something for you as well as for herself. Apart from thinking you a terrific actress, she thought it was all so terribly unfair, when you didn't even know Jon and had no reason at all for wanting him dead. She could be genuine."

"I don't believe it!" Aidan and Ruth exclaimed in unison.

Judith raised a brow in Aidan's direction. "Why else should she want to get in touch with Ruth?"

"Don't ask me," he said.

Ruth fingered the scar left by the gash on her arm until she became aware of Aidan's eyes on her. "Did she actually ask for my address?" she said thoughtfully.

Judith shrugged. "She asked if you were in London, or if you'd gone to ground until the gossip blew over. She wanted to get in touch with you."

"You see," Ruth went on in carefully noncommittal tones, "I think she already knew my address. She knew it because she knew her aunt had left me a cottage on Lindisfarne when she died."

"Her *aunt*?" Judith nearly roared. "Your reclusive Miss Moir?"

"The very same," said Ruth.

Chapter Eight

Ruth came back from the rehearsal for the advertisement content that Judith, as usual, had been right. The part was made for her. Ruth had always had a natural gift for comedy and she enjoyed playing the harebrained heroine, preparing to go out with her boyfriend. The plot was simple; the bathwater is cold; Ruth's hair dryer blows up in her hand; everything goes wrong! But as soon as she turns to the new beauty product—kind to both people and animals—order is magically restored and her boyfriend is duly impressed and asks for her hand in marriage as soon as he comes in the door.

It was Sunday morning when Ruth told Judith over breakfast that she would sign up for the whole series of advertisements.

"They're not paying all that well," Judith warned her, spreading her piece of toast with marmalade.

"Beggars can't be choosers. Besides, the scripts are well written and great fun. You were right when you said they'd be good for me. There couldn't be a more sympathetic role for me to make my comeback in.''

''That's what I thought,'' Judith admitted. ''The sponsors will be watching the response of the public as eagerly as we shall be.'' She made a face as a dollop of marmalade landed on the tablecloth. ''However, don't let's start worrying about that now!''

''It's work—that's all I care about right now,'' Ruth answered with feeling. ''I don't mind telling you that I'd have taken a far less sympathetic part than this one, just for the joy of earning some money again.''

''Bad as that?''

Ruth nodded. ''I don't know what I would have done without Miss Moir's cottage.''

The front door bell rang. ''Answer it, will you, Ruth? I'm going to get dressed. Who on earth could be visiting this time of day on a Sunday?''

Ruth knew who it was before she even opened the door. She tried not to smile a welcome to him, but she couldn't help herself as Aidan came into view. ''Hullo there,'' she greeted him.

''Hullo yourself.''

He beckoned to her and she leaned towards him, still holding the doorknob. He bent his head and kissed her on the lips.

''Judith doesn't think this a civilized hour to call,'' she reproved him gravely.

''Too early?''

''We were just having breakfast. Judith has gone to get dressed—''

''I didn't come to see Judith.''

Ruth turned away, leaving him to shut the door behind himself as he followed her into the tiny, pretty kitchen.

"Give the man some coffee," Judith called out to her from her bedroom.

Ruth raised questioning eyebrows at Aidan. "Coffee?" she asked him.

He seated himself beside her at the shelf that served as a place to eat in the kitchen. "I like having breakfast with you. How come you're already dressed?"

"I went to church."

He considered that, turning it over in his mind, deciding that the thought of her in church gave him pleasure. Hardly anyone he knew ever bothered these days, yet it obviously meant something to Ruth.

"D'you go often?"

"She goes every week," Judith answered for her, appearing suddenly in the kitchen, "don't you, love?"

Ruth didn't answer, but shrugged shyly. She poured out the coffee into three mugs and pushed them towards the others. Aidan accepted his with a smile. "Is this all we're having?" he asked.

Ruth took a sip of the hot liquid. "Did you come just for breakfast or did you have another reason?" she countered.

"I thought if you gave me breakfast, I'd give you lunch and dinner. You, too, Judith!"

"Thank you, but no," Judith replied at once. "I use Sundays to catch up on the rest of the week and do all my paperwork. Take Ruth, by all means. She's already missing Lindisfarne and complaining there's no air in London."

"There isn't," Aidan agreed. "But I know where we can find some. When did you last take a trip along the river?"

Ruth wasn't sure of the wisdom of accepting the invitation, no matter how much Judith urged her to go and enjoy herself. She wanted to go too badly. She had thought she might view Aidan differently, once she was back at work again and doing the thing that mattered to her most in the

world. She saw that that had been a delusion. The sight of
Aidan at the front door had brought back the feeling that
had come to life in Lindisfarne. Her whole being had
jumped for joy, her heart doing acrobatics and knocking
against her ribs when he smiled that special smile she was
coming to know so well.

"It may rain," Ruth began.

"Windsor," Aidan said solemnly, "is like Camelot. It
only rains on the appointed day of the week, which isn't
Sunday."

"Fool," Ruth said fondly. "It rains everywhere on a
Sunday."

"Come and see?"

"All right."

Judith made some toast and gestured towards several
brands of cereals for Aidan to choose from. As far as she
was concerned, that was breakfast catered for, and she retired to the living room and a more comfortable chair to
glance through the Sunday papers. She came to again,
however, to see the two of them off, saying in an aside to
Ruth. "He's too good to waste. Enjoy yourself with him.
It'll do your work good—if you can't think of a better reason for yourself!"

It was raining as Ruth and Aidan set foot on the ferry, but
it didn't seem to matter. A disembodied voice called their
attention to the various historic buildings on either bank as
they went slowly up the river. Ruth gave her full attention
to the sites, frowning as she tried to make out each place that
was mentioned. Aidan didn't pretend to be interested. He
watched her expressive features instead, enjoying the pleasure he saw written there. They came upon the country
reaches farther up river and passed through one lock after
another, smaller crafts darting in and out alongside them.

"I've never been on the river before," Ruth confessed, becoming aware of his eyes on her. She was a little embarrassed to be watched so closely and felt suddenly foolish, as if her enthusiasm were a bit childish.

"What do you do with yourself?" Aidan asked, sounding shocked.

She blinked, not looking at him. "I work."

"Sundays too?"

"Charity work comes on Sundays. It's another way of getting known."

He knew her better now than to think that was why she did it. "Sundays are for friends and family. A few precious hours *we* can spend together every week—"

"Every week?" she repeated sharply.

"Why not?"

There wasn't any reason that she thought would satisfy him. She gave him a meaningful look instead. "You'd soon get bored of that."

"No, darling, I would not. And don't play-act with me." He grinned wryly. "I know when you're playing a part and when you're not. Difficult though you'll find this to believe, I much prefer the woman herself to any performance you'll ever give—on the boards or off them."

Ruth was more embarrassed than ever. It wasn't the first time she had felt naked before him. She would have liked to be angry with him, but she wasn't, and it was too much trouble to pretend an emotion she was far from feeling—especially if he could tell the difference.

"Don't," she said instead, catching her lower lip between her teeth.

He put an arm round her shoulders and hugged her. "I have a plan. If I stick around for long enough, you'll grow used to me being here—you might even get fond of me. And then we'll pass on to the next stage."

"What's that?" she asked cautiously.

"Wait and see."

Miraculously, the sun came out just as Windsor Castle came into view. Of all the castles in the world, there could be few as romantic as that huge palace, golden and magnificent in the yellow sunlight. Beside it flowed the river, the leafy trees a shimmer of green, made brighter by the deeper green-brown of the water.

"It's enormous!" Ruth exclaimed.

"Impressive," Aidan agreed. "I imagine it must be a nice place to live, on the whole. I shouldn't like the air traffic from Heathrow going overhead all the time though, would you?"

"There are drawbacks to everything," Ruth said with the frank envy of one who would never expect to live in a castle.

Royal Windsor lived up to every expectation. They wandered through the streets, finding a place to eat overlooking the river and the bridge that crossed it leading to Eton. A good many of the Eton schoolboys, "young gentlemen," had chosen the same restaurant for Sunday lunch with their parents. Ruth and Aidan observed as they languidly entertained their awkward parents with stories of their doings, evidently convinced that they, and only they, had the key to successful living.

"Were you like that when you were at school?" Ruth asked Aidan.

"I didn't go to Eton."

"Where did you go?"

He looked apologetic. "Winchester."

"Ah. Where the *clever* ones go," she said knowledgeably. She knew that from a play she had been in. "A bit different from my old school."

"Very. You didn't have to run round a hill every morning, or have cold baths, or suffer from the chill of no glass in the windows, or any other of the monastic refinements of the British public school system. It's a barbaric system," Aidan said, only half-joking.

"It seems to turn out some quite nice people," Ruth remarked.

"Is that a compliment?" He looked as pleased as if she had handed him a bouquet.

"Won't you send your sons to Winchester?" Ruth inquired, in an effort to distract him.

"No, I don't think I shall. I'd rather give them other things. They'll be somebody else's sons as well as mine, after all, and *she* may have strong ideas about their schooling, also."

Too late, she saw the laughter in his eyes and saw the possible implication behind his words. She changed the subject with a promptness that was gauche, especially with someone as observant as she knew him to be. "Jonathan Ross made his name producing advertisements for television. Did you know that? I'm hoping great things from this series, especially as they're bound to be played a lot before Christmas."

He took his cue from her. "*Christmas?* I refuse to discuss anything to do with Christmas in the middle of summer."

"One has to plan ahead," she pointed out.

"Especially when it comes to the education of our children," Aidan retorted with a completely straight face.

She opened her eyes wide, determined to have her revenge. "How do you know I want any?" she demanded.

He was laughing as he called for the bill, and was still laughing when he helped her on with her jacket.

She was inclined to be indignant. "Children don't fit in with my career."

"My dearest darling, other actresses seem to manage. We won't embark on a family until you're good and ready, however. Will that do?"

Her heartbeat pounded in her ears. "What's this *we* bit? There isn't any 'we'—" She broke off, panic setting in as she tried not to look at him. She felt as if she were fighting, single-handed, against the inevitability of the tide coming in. She had as little chance of winning with this man. Worse, she wasn't sure she wanted to win!

"Come home with me and I'll show you some of the advantages of being a 'we'."

The wicked devilment on his face was nearly her undoing. "You're inviting me to see your etchings, I presume?" she mocked him.

"Why not? I've seen yours."

"My etchings?"

"Watercolours, etchings, same difference." He shrugged his shoulders convivially. "Let's go and look at some of the Queen's while we make up our minds."

A light drizzle greeted them outside, which made the visit to Windsor Castle all the more attractive. Above the ramparts flew the Royal Standard, proclaiming that the monarch was in residence, as she frequently was on weekends. It seemed a fitting emblem, tying England's past to her future, as did the heraldic devices of the Knights of the Garter that were kept above the Knights' Stalls in St. George's Chapel.

Ruth enjoyed the afternoon more than any other she could remember. Aidan knew it, too. As they stepped back on board the ferry for Tower Bridge, he put his hand on her shoulder and whispered in her ear: "How's Miss Independence doing now?"

"She's alive and kicking," Ruth maintained firmly.

He kissed her cheek. "That's good to know."

Her glance was sober. "I thought you wanted—"

"I don't want to take anything away from you, dear heart. There's more to life, not less, when you have a partner. Has being happy with me made you less of an actress?"

"There was no conflict of interest this afternoon," she answered dryly. "Wait until there is. The woman always loses. She's expected to. Will you give up any of your cases because I've got a part on Broadway?"

"Probably not."

"Well then?" Ruth asked sadly.

"I'd rather be parted from you from time to time than not have you at all."

"How do you know you can trust me when I'm on the other side of the world?" she threw at him, considerably put-out to discover that the thought of being away from him even for a few weeks was more than she could bear to contemplate. It was already too late for them to be having this argument.

His look made her face burn. "How do I know I can trust you?" she blurted out defensively.

"I can't help you with that. I can't prove it to you. Either you do trust me or you don't."

She wished she could meet his honesty with her own. Honesty meant respect. But it didn't make her feel any better to know that she could trust him to be honest. She was all mixed up inside, half of her wanting to run from him while she still could, the other half already so deeply in love with him that she knew it was too late for her to escape. He had sprung the tender trap on her and she might just as well admit it.

It was right and fitting for them to step off the ferry beside the Tower of London, the oldest of the royal palaces. A couple of wardens, dressed in their Tudor uniforms, stood beside the entrance. They looked like the court figures on a pack of cards, saved from being ridiculous only by what they represented, a continuity of life that stretched back over the centuries.

"Do you mind wearing a wig and gown when you appear in court?" Ruth asked Aidan.

"No. It feels proper somehow. One wonders, though, if tradition isn't sometimes taken too far in this country. Wigs, and all the other trappings of the past don't make up for a bad presentation of the client's case."

Aidan didn't ask again if Ruth wanted to see where he lived. He took it for granted that she was going home with him and, she admitted to herself, she had taken it for granted as well. She wanted to see his home, *needed* to see it if she wanted to know him better.

Even so, it surprised her when he opened the door for her and pushed her through it ahead of him into the tiny hall of his apartment. She could see directly into the living room. There was a comfortable leather-covered sofa and two chairs grouped at one end, a rosewood dining table at the other, surrounded by a set of antique carvers in which one could relax comfortably over a meal in the continental manner. Together with the jade-green curtains and white carpet, this was one of the most pleasing rooms she had ever been in.

"Like it?"

"Love it! Did you inherit all this furniture?"

"My parents gave me the leather chairs; the rest I bought and paid for myself. I earn a fair paycheck these days. I can keep you in something better than penury."

"I know that." Ruth was afraid she might have hurt his feelings. She hadn't intended that. She had wanted to know what it felt like to be part of a loving family when it came to setting up one's own home. "I'm hardly earning anything at the moment. Aren't you afraid I might find your money a temptation?"

"No, my prickly friend, I am not," Aidan said, smiling confidently.

She set her mouth in a stubborn line. "I like nice things. I love this room."

"Come and see the bedroom," he invited her.

The king-size bed was a problem to her. Ruth tried not to stare at it, imagining all sorts of things that were none of her business. The biggest shock of all was that she, who had spent her whole life without a care in the world as to what anyone else was doing, was eaten up with jealousy when she thought of that bed. Nobody, not even someone of Aidan's size, needed a king-size bed all to himself.

Her look round the fitted furniture and the printed curtains, chosen, Aidan told her, by his mother, was cursory in the extreme. She was far too busy maintaining control over her facial expression in case he should guess what she was really feeling. It was humiliating to her that she should be in such a state over nothing at all.

"What about the kitchen?" Ruth asked.

Aidan grinned at her—a slow, knowing grin that made her scalp prickle. Dammit, he knew. He knew exactly what seeing his bedroom was doing to her. He had shown it to her with that in mind!

"The kitchen," she said again, more firmly.

"Well," he began doubtfully, "I don't want you to think that I'll ever suppose it to be your proper place in my home—"

Ruth glowered at him. He had already made it abundantly clear where he considered her place to be.

"I want to see the kitchen," she said a bit too loudly.

He folded his arms across his chest, still grinning like a Cheshire cat. "What makes you think you'll feel any safer in the kitchen?"

She should never have come. If anything had been needed to convince her, this was was it—she should run while she still could! Ruth glanced at her watch, wondering how frequently the buses ran on a Sunday evening from the City. With her luck, they probably didn't run at all. Very well, she would walk—at least, she would walk until she spied a taxi—and then she would take the cab for the rest of the way, never mind what it cost her. She was making money again. She *deserved* to be able to take a taxi.

"See the kitchen first and then I'll take you home," Aidan said.

She looked at him with unseeing eyes, the panic still surging within her. To her amazement, he held out a hand to her and she found herself taking it, clutching at him for comfort.

"Why do you have such a large bed?" she heard herself asking.

He smiled deep into her eyes. "Does it frighten you? I'm a big fellow and I take up a lot of room. I shouldn't mind sharing a smaller bed with you, though, if that's what you want."

She shook herself, suddenly wanting to smile back at him, to whoop it up, to laugh and sing; even to invite him to kiss her and never mind the consequences! "I have a confession to make," she began shyly. "Right now, I wouldn't mind—"

"You're not experienced enough to make such an awesome decision without trying it out. You'd better come and inspect the kitchen before you spoil your good record, my girl," Aidan said quite seriously.

It was like a kick under the ribs. She stared at him in consternation. "I think at thirty I can make up my own mind," Ruth said with dignity.

"I haven't seen much evidence of that!"

"You don't want me?" she accused, feeling more and more flustered.

"I want you," he murmured, his eyes smoldering.

Ruth was confused by what he'd said. What was he doing showing her the bedroom if he hadn't wanted... The thought sank in that Aidan might really mean what he'd said to her about courting. Quickly, Ruth blurted. "I want you, too."

Aidan's eyes widened. Then, congenially, he kissed her on the end of her nose. "That's the nicest thing that's ever been said to me. I can't say I'm not tempted. But making love isn't something I want you to regret. Come and look at the kitchen and then I'll take you home."

"You promised me dinner," she reminded him, the disappointment at not having been kissed a bitter taste in her mouth.

"I haven't forgotten. I had it in mind to feed you here, but we'll go out. And don't argue. I want more than a couple of nights of love with you. A lifetime of you won't be enough for me."

Ruth shook her head, not knowing what to say. Her fine eyes sparkled with tears. There was no pretence about her now; he had stripped the tools of her trade away from her. "I may disappoint you," she said at last, afraid it was all too good to be true. "I've never loved or been loved. I don't know anything about family life. I don't know how to share—"

"How do you know?"

She loved him for his gentleness. "I think it's something one has to learn as a child. I never did."

He led the way into the neatly fitted kitchen, where everything was to hand. The tears brimmed over her eyes and ran unchecked down her cheeks. She watched in silence as he pulled out cabinets, showed off the hob and the latest model in ovens. At last he came to a stop.

"Sweetheart, we've already shared one kitchen and we managed very well together."

"Emotions are something different," she sniffed.

"Are they?"

She suspected he was laughing at her again, but Ruth didn't mind. She stamped her foot. "I want to be kissed here and now."

Willingly, he took her into his arms. "A few kisses can't hurt," he agreed, "but I'm going to take you home before it develops into anything more. Is it a bargain?"

She nodded her head. There was a painful catch to her breath as she forced herself to relax against him. She'd been kissed before—many, many times, on film, on stage, before the TV cameras—and it had meant nothing to her. Now she was as nervous as a kitten as his fingers explored the line of her jaw. She had a good view of his face, the tender curve of his lips, the solemn worship in his eyes. Did he love her? She had no way of knowing.

His fingers toyed with the buttons of her bodice, undoing them just as his lips met hers. After that, it was like entering a new world of experience. His tongue met hers, encouraging her to experiment on her own account. With increasing delight, she made herself familiar with the taste and smell of him, overcome by the beauty of the man who seemed to be finding a like pleasure from holding and touching her.

When he finally drew away, she saw the hot passion in his eyes and could not doubt that he wanted her. Belatedly, she realized that she was naked to the waist. Yesterday she would have covered herself immediately, but today was different and if it pleased him to see her like that, it was giving her far more to know that she was the object of that desire. Her nipples hardened, longing again for his touch. With regret, he closed her bodice, his eyes warm and enticing as he looked deep into hers. "You know why I'm taking you home?"

Again Ruth nodded, now beyond speech. Aidan gave her a last, swift kiss on the lips—a kiss quite different from his earlier ones, but no less sweet to her for its very gentleness.

He looked round the kitchen, taking deep breaths to calm himself. "I'll never feel quite the same about this kitchen," he said at last. "Your ghost will be here even when I'm eating my cornflakes for breakfast. Do you realize what you've done to me?"

She found herself smiling. "Shackles of gold?" She held out her wrists for his inspection. "A matching pair to the ones you've put on me."

"Do you mind?"

"No woman minds being given jewelry," she said smiling.

He laughed. "Oh, darling, I wish I didn't have to take you home."

"I do too."

But Ruth went with him meekly enough, picking up her jacket as they went out, knowing she would never be the same person again. She might look the same, be wearing the same clothes, but there was a glow that had never lit her face in quite that way before, and a warm confidence in herself that had been lacking all her life. She felt, quite simply, as though she had come home.

Ruth and Aidan stood together in the cavernous parking area under the block of flats where Aidan kept his car. Ruth could well do without the place. She didn't like the closed-in feeling it gave her.

"I'll just fetch the car and bring it around," he said, giving her one of his bright smiles.

"I'll wait for you outside," she said, as he stepped into the lift.

Aidan nodded his agreement, still elated that Ruth had told him she loved him. "I shan't be long." The doors closed before him.

Ruth watched the yellow lights of the lift disappear below before she turned away, walking slowly across the public foyer towards the self-opening glass doors. Her heels sounded on the floor. The silence all about her was so great that she was tempted to walk on tiptoe until she gained the street outside.

Then, just as she reached the doors, a hand caught at her sleeve, pulling her off balance. To her astonishment, Ruth saw it was Sylvia Ross.

"What are you doing here?" Ruth asked her, fixing a smile onto her face.

"Oh, I'm just visiting. One of my closest friends lives here. I think you know him. Aidan Wakefield?" Malice was written on Sylvia's pale face. "But of course you know him," she went on with a giggle. "He was going to be your barrister, wasn't he? I have the advantage of knowing him in his *private* life."

"Really?" Ruth did her best to quell the rush of jealousy and suspicion that was threatening to undermine her hard-won confidence in Aidan. In response to her query Sylvia gave her a patronizing look.

"Between you and me," Sylvia said, her tone biting, "Jonathan wasn't the only man in my life from the moment we got married. Aidan is so much more exciting than my poor Jon ever was."

Ruth felt slightly sick. "You're looking very well, Sylvia," she said.

"A *very* merry widow!" Sylvia agreed, teeth glinting, with another giggle.

Ruth favoured her with a sour grimace. "What were you doing on Lindisfarne?"

Sylvia's laugh tinkled. "Need you ask? Wasn't Aidan up there, too?"

"I suppose you know Mrs. Jenkins too?"

"Eileen? How could I help but know her? I used to visit with my aunt whenever I could, I'll have you know."

That wasn't Mrs. Jenkins's story, but Ruth wasn't going to argue right now. "Indeed?" Ruth tossed off doing her best to show Sylvia she didn't care what she said. "Lovely to see you, Sylvia. Good-bye."

Ruth walked out the door, her head held high, and saw that Aidan's car was already drawn up to the curb outside. She went slowly down the steps towards him, trying to dismiss from her mind all that Sylvia had implied and recapture the golden mood Aidan had brought into her life.

She never made it to the bottom of the steps. There was a blow to the back of her head, her knees buckled, and Ruth fell heavily to the pavement below. She heard a scream of pain, not realizing that it came from her own throat, and then knew no more.

Chapter Nine

The bright lights bothered her. Ruth put up a hand to shield her eyes, uttering a muddled protest as someone pulled down her lower lid and shone yet another light straight into her eye.

"She'll do. Must have a harder head than we gave her credit for."

"Can I take her home?" That voice was Aidan's. Ruth froze. *Aidan and Sylvia together?*

"I don't want to go anywhere!" she said aloud.

"Quite right, young lady. I'll take another look at you tomorrow and we can think about your going home then."

Where was she now? Ruth struggled to open her eyes and look about her, but the effort was too much for her.

"Where's Sylvia?" she croaked, feeling an ache in her head.

Neither man bothered to answer her. A nurse tidied the bedclothes with a professional friendliness that made her aware of the aching loneliness that had engulfed her when

Sylvia had mentioned Aidan. So what was new? Ruth was on her own again. And someone was trying to murder her!

"If Sylvia comes here, I can't see her."

The loudness of her own voice made her head ache more. An instant later, Aidan's face came swimming into sight.

"What's this about Sylvia? Did you see her?"

Her smile was so wry it was scarcely a smile at all. It didn't hide her fear and hurt. "As if you didn't know," she said.

"*Hinny*, what are you talking about?"

"Don't call me that!" Ruth ground out, rolling onto her side so that her back was to him and feeling as though she were wrenching her heart out in the process. She screwed her eyes tightly shut, not minding that it hurt and hoping she was hurt badly enough to die—to die quickly, before the full horror of what he had done to her seeped into her conscious mind.

Aidan turned back to the doctor, shrugging his shoulders. "I thought she fell over when the heel of her shoe broke. Could someone have pushed her, doctor?"

"Sylvia hit me over the head!"

Aidan turned back to Ruth. "Sylvia did? Are you sure of that, my love?" She lifted an impatient arm, waving him away, and the scar she had received in an earlier encounter with violence was plainly visible. "Sylvia Ross?" Aidan mused.

"When are you going to make her Sylvia Wakefield?" Ruth asked bitterly.

Aidan started. He walked round the bed, frowning threateningly down at her. "You, more than anyone, ought to know the answer to that."

Ruth blinked. Her eyes stung as though she were about to cry, but there were no tears there. She was hurting far too badly for tears.

"I don't know. I thought I did—but I don't understand at all. I didn't even know she was a friend of yours!"

"She isn't!"

"Then why does she visit you so often?"

"Visit me?"

"Go away," Ruth cried, too tired and hurt to face him now.

"Okay, I'm going. I'll be back for you in the morning and we'll talk then—"

"Judith is coming for me."

Sadly, Aidan put his fingers to his lips, kissed them, and transferred the kiss to her mouth. "Judith doesn't know you're in here yet, darling. I'll ask her to come with me in the morning."

"No! Tell her to come on her own," Ruth watched Aidan storm out of the room and out of her life forever.

Sometime after he had gone, the nurse gently washed her face. Sitting on the edge of her bed, the woman ran a cool cloth over Ruth's forehead.

"If that man were mine, I'd go falling over my own feet, too," she said in tones that implied Ruth didn't deserve her good fortune. "Some people have all the luck. When he takes you home tomorrow, he'll kiss it better, and you'll forget you ever had to spend a night here."

"That man had me hit over the head," Ruth told her dryly.

"I guess it could feel like that," the nurse sighed. Then she laughed. "I'll have to tell my boyfriend that one. All right, I think you'll do," she said, finishing up. "Want something to help you sleep? I'll get the doctor to write it up for you before he disappears again."

Ruth accepted the small blue pill with relief. She didn't want to think any more that day. She wanted to sleep and never wake up again. She wanted—Aidan! Even now, knowing she couldn't trust him, she still wanted him.

When she opened her eyes, a shaft of moonlight streamed across her bed. One of the other patients in the ward was stirring also. Ruth tried to sleep again, but she found it difficult with other people in the room. Her head hurt. She hurt all over! Silently, the tears began to come, not the healing tears that she had hoped for, but hideous, painful tears that were wrenched out of her as if by hammer blows.

"Is there anything wrong, dear?" Her fellow patient stood like a wraith in the moonlight, breathing heavily with the effort of walking across the ward.

"No, I'm all right," Ruth whispered back.

"You looked so awful when you were brought in, I was afraid for you. Whatever did you do?"

"Fell down some steps."

"That isn't what they said when they saw you. The rumour was you'd been mugged. You didn't have a handbag with you, you see. Has it been found yet?"

"I don't know," Ruth admitted.

"Never mind, love. That man of yours will look after you. Almost worth it to be carried about by him, if you know what I mean."

Ruth smiled, but was not reassured. The lady had no idea how Aidan had betrayed her. She supposed that from the outside, he would appear a concerned friend, perhaps more than that. Ruth only wished she could believe it was true.

By the time morning came, Ruth's greatest ambition was to get out of the place.

"You'd better wait for your fiancé," she was told over and over again. The nurses and doctors paid no attention when she denied she had a fiancé, even less when she said she was afraid to go anywhere with him. Aidan had done a good job of making himself popular with the whole staff. Nobody was going to believe he was in league with Sylvia Ross and plotting to have her murdered.

"The only person I want to see is Judith Tate, my agent," she insisted. "I'm afraid of Aidan Wakefield. Isn't that enough for you?"

They were kind and very professional. "If you'd seen the state he was in when he brought you here, you wouldn't think he wished you any harm, dear."

"I'm taking myself home by taxi," Ruth had insisted.

The whole ward followed this exchange with round-eyed interest. "I thought I recognized you, love," the old lady of the midnight visit said in triumph. "Seen you on the telly I have. I suppose—will you give me your autograph before you go? I pretend I want them for my granddaughter, but I don't mind telling you that I've been a collector for years and years. Is that young man of yours an actor, too?"

"No. He's a lawyer."

"Never mind him then, I'll make do with you. The last time I saw you, you were playing a nurse, and now here we are together in hospital! Strange how life works out, isn't it?"

Ruth agreed that it was. She signed her name on a card, pleased to be asked. Here was one member of the public, at least, who knew nothing of the recent scandal with Jonathan Ross. She wondered if she and Judith hadn't overrated the damage it had done her career. Perhaps nobody really cared at all. Why should they if they weren't personally involved?

Ruth signed her name again on the hospital release. She then forced herself into her clothes, took the lift downstairs and collapsed into the first empty taxicab that came along, giving the driver Judith's address with such a guilty look that he was in two minds as to whether it was safe to take her anywhere.

Judith was at home and quite hysterical. She paid for the cab and immediately began berating Ruth.

"Where have you been? I rang the hospital and they said you'd insisted on leaving, despite all their warnings that you might have a delayed reaction to the fall. Are you mad? You may be concussed—anything!"

"I'm not."

"How do *you* know?"

"If there had been any danger of that, they would have come along every couple of hours and woken me, probably peering into my eyes—"

"You can't know that!"

"I do know. They did that in *The Casualty Ward*, remember?"

"That was on television. This is real life."

"If I'd stayed, they'd have kept me there until Aidan came for me," Ruth said abruptly. "I couldn't take that risk."

"My dear girl, Aidan was here half the night, carrying on about you, how he should never have left you alone—"

"The acting profession lost quite a performer when he decided to take up law, didn't it?" Ruth said dryly.

"Ruth!"

Ruth shrugged her shoulders. She couldn't say anything more about Aidan. Her mouth felt stiff, as if it didn't quite belong to her. Come to think of it, her whole body felt a bit like that. She felt terrible! She must have looked it, too, for Judith pushed her into the nearest chair and brought her a cup of tea almost before she had turned round.

"The English panacea," Ruth said glumly. She wasn't really very fond of tea, preferring coffee—in the mornings, at least.

Judith added sugar to her own cup. "I'm in need of it, even if you're not. Are you trying to tell me that Aidan has something to do with all this?"

Ruth nodded, dispirited. "Sylvia Ross is an old friend of his."

"Did he tell you that?"

"No, she did."

Judith was completely knocked off balance. "I don't believe it! *When* did she tell you that?"

"Before she hit me over the head and pushed me down the steps yesterday. Charming pair, aren't they?"

"Ruth, you can't be thinking that. I wouldn't believe a word that woman said. I'm convinced she's mad. What did she hope to gain by hitting you over the head in the first place?"

Ruth took a sip of tea and said softly, "I think she meant to kill me."

Judith's horrified look made Ruth want to laugh. Once she started, however, she knew she wouldn't be able to stop. She dug her teeth into her lower lip, pushing the hysteria back where it belonged.

"I ought to be at work. I can't go looking like this. Will they be able to find someone else at such short notice?"

Immediately, Judith was the professional woman again, in charge of herself and the situation. "You don't have to worry about that. I rang them up earlier. Fortunately, the rushes yesterday were so good that they're prepared to wait for you."

"They must have been good."

Judith's exasperation boiled over. "They were lucky to get you! I can't think what it is with you, Ruth, you never have had any idea of your own worth. It niggles me, especially as I *know* you're one of the few who'll probably end up with a handle to your name. Dame Ruth Gaynor. How does that sound to you?''

"It would be fun to meet the Queen," Ruth mused.

"Is that all?"

"But I'd like to. Really I would."

"Wouldn't we all? What are you going to do now?"

Ruth thought about it. "I'm going to hire myself a solicitor to find out what was really in Miss Moir's will."

Judith gave her a sidelong glance. "Yes, but, you're not the first person to think of that. Aidan was here at some ungodly hour, breathing fire down his nostrils and muttering that the key to everything had to be in that 'darned will.' He said he was going to get to the bottom of it all before you came out of the safety of a hospital ward. How little he knows you."

"All he had to do was ask Sylvia. I bet she'd know the will backwards."

"Perhaps they're not such good friends as you think." Judith regarded Ruth over the rim of her cup. "I like Aidan. I think he's good for you—"

"He put me in hospital!"

"I don't believe that."

"You weren't there," Ruth said sadly.

In the end, though, Ruth never went to hire a solicitor at all. Judith suggested in an offhand way, which wouldn't have deceived a child, that she go and lie down for a bit. "You look terrible. If worst comes to worst, I'll go and get you a copy of the will myself." She gazed thoughtfully into space for a moment. "Or my secretary will, poor girl. She's had a lot to put up with recently."

That Ruth could believe. If it hadn't been for Judith's work, she didn't think she would have survived the past few months.

"Tell her thanks from me," she said.

Judith smiled. "Think nothing of it. When you get your gong, I'll still be there as your agent—the whole office knows that."

Once she had been prevailed upon to lie down in Judith's spare room, Ruth fell fast asleep. She was still half-asleep when she smelled something cooking in the kitchen. Even before she was awake, Ruth felt the first pangs of hunger. She was starving!

The book Ruth had been reading fell onto the rug as she put her feet on the floor. The very pretty bookmark had been crocheted for her the first time she had appeared at Stratford-upon-Avon by an eighty-four-year-old Shakespearian fan who could recite all the plays better than Olivier. That had been a good day, one of the most exciting in her life, when she had known with a kind of golden certainty that what she wanted to do more than anything else in the world was to bring such plays to life. She felt perhaps that dream might come true. But as to her others...

Now she wanted Aidan and she couldn't have him.

In the kitchen, Aidan stood by the stove, cooking.

Ruth was frozen with fear in the doorway. Sooner or later, he was bound to turn and see her, and then what? Would he kill her? Would he pretend still to be in love with her? She didn't think she could stand it if he did. She wanted him so badly that she ached with her need for him. But she didn't trust him. She never would again.

"Hungry?"

Ruth nearly jumped out of her skin. "What are you doing here?" Her voice came out as a whisper.

"Cooking lunch."

"Does Judith know?"

"Know I'm here? She gave me the key. She's worried about you—"

"But not about you?"

"I wasn't batted over the head."

Ruth could feel herself breaking up inside. Surely, she thought, she wasn't going to dissolve into tears now, just when she needed to keep her wits about her? *Oh, Aidan!*

"I thought you'd decided I fell over my own feet," she challenged him.

He slapped a plate down on the counter, pointing to the chair in front of it. "Sit down and eat. I'm very nearly at the end of my patience, Ruth Gaynor. What was anyone to think when one moment you were tripping lightly down the steps towards me and the next you were sprawled out on the pavement. How you women can wear such instruments of torture is beyond me."

Ruth sat. "They make our feet and ankles look good. Haven't you noticed?"

He took a deep breath. "On other women, yes. When I look at you, I look at you, not at the shapeliness of your ankles."

She took refuge behind putting some baked beans into her mouth. Funny, she had always thought she didn't much care for baked beans, and yet, here she was, putting them away as though she hadn't eaten anything for days!

"I'll tell you what kind of woman you are," he went on smoothly. "You're a timid little thing, with no great opinion of yourself, who doesn't think she deserves any personal happiness, and who's afraid of putting it on the line that she's fallen for just the right man for her—"

"I want a career, not a man."

"Oh no, not that again."

Ruth sniffed, eating her baked beans. "Judith manages without a man," she said at last.

"Have you ever asked her why?"

Ruth never had. The subject had never come up between them. Judith was older than she was, and a manager besides. She was a born agent, keeping all her clients on the straight and narrow, pushing their careers along the paths that she mapped out for them. Judith was her friend, but she was also a mother-figure, though Ruth had never thought of her as that before. "Are you trying to tell me something?" Ruth demanded.

Aidan put down his own plate and sat down beside her. "Judith was widowed almost before she was married. He was killed in Zimbabwe—Rhodesia as it was then. He happened to be in the wrong place at the wrong time, travelling in a train up Africa. He was killed by a stray bullet in an ambush."

Ruth was shocked. "I never knew that."

"Judith thinks you have troubles enough, without adding hers to your burden."

"But you don't think like that, do you?" Ruth murmured.

"No."

She turned and looked at him then. "Why not?"

"It's all part of the family life you crave. If you belong to a family you can't help caring about the other members. It's the same with friends. You care about Judith's happiness, don't you?"

Ruth looked down at her empty plate. "Obviously she doesn't think so."

"Of course she does, you noodle. What she *doesn't* understand is that you don't recognize the smoke signals one member of a family sends up to the others when they want help, or solitude, or company, or whatever else we need."

Ruth was more bewildered than ever. "I don't?"

"No, which is why I've decided to take your education in hand—in the nicest way, of course—"

"Of course," Ruth said, still confused.

He balanced his last bean on his fork and grinned at her. "You don't have a clue how I feel about you, do you?"

"No," she admitted.

"And look at all the smoke signals I've been sending up!" he mourned.

"What about Sylvia Ross?" she retorted.

"You tell me," he returned calmly. "What about Sylvia Ross?"

"She knows where you live."

"My address is in the telephone book."

"She said she visited you *often*!"

"And you believed her?"

Ruth gave him a quick, sidelong glance, followed by a reluctant smile. "I'm glad I'm not in the witness box," she said wryly.

He still looked on the dejected side, she thought. It was obvious he had managed to convince Judith he was to be trusted—but Judith hadn't been there last night.

"Whom else was she waiting for if it wasn't you?" she demanded.

"It could have been you," Aidan said.

Ruth made a face. "My head still aches from that meeting!"

"It could have been worse," he said softly. "You could have been dead."

For the first time she noticed he was as pale as she had been when she last saw her face in the glass. Ruth shifted uncomfortably in her seat.

"Tell me about last night," Aidan continued.

"You were there."

He shook his head. "Tell me from the moment I stepped onto the lift—from when you were on your own."

"I watched the lift disappear," she began. "I walked towards the doors. Sylvia came up behind me, pulling on my sleeve. She said she was there visiting you—"

"As she often did?"

Ruth bit her lip. "Yes."

"Then what happened?"

"I started off down the steps and she must have hit me over the head. That's all I know. When I woke up, I was in hospital."

"Interesting. Would you be prepared to brave Sylvia Ross once more?"

Ruth breathed deeply. "Do you want my death on your conscience?"

Aidan gazed at her with brooding eyes, almost as though he disliked her, or as if she were some ghastly puzzle he was determined to solve.

"I want this to be over!" he answered her. "I hadn't realized how much easier it is to be a barrister than a policeman—or a man in love with the victim."

"With Sylvia?" she shot at him.

To her astonishment, Aidan blew his top. It was one of the most marvellous moments of her life. Ruth listened to the words coming out of his mouth, a great stream of invective, beginning with the first moment he had seen her and ending with his feelings when he had picked her up off the pavement the night before and had carried her into the hospital.

"And I hadn't even kissed you good-night," he added for good measure. "I could wring your neck!"

Her mouth dropped open. "I daresay Sylvia didn't think of that."

"No imagination!"

She laughed. "I had a miserable night," she told him. "I felt so alone."

"You didn't trust me," he accused.

"No. I wanted to, Aidan, but Sylvia was very convincing and I'm not used to relying on anyone else for anything. Why wouldn't you prefer Sylvia, after all? You have a lot more to gain from her!"

He stood beside her, leaning down so that his head was level with hers. "I'm going to tell you only once, so listen carefully, my love. We have other things to do today. Are you listening? *Really* listening?"

Ruth nodded, her eyes wide.

"Well then, you're the most exciting woman who's ever come my way. Sometimes you look so ordinary and lost it breaks my heart, and then, with a single movement, you're a raving beauty—the most marvellous temptation to any man since Helen of Troy. You're prickly, easy to hurt, and haven't the slightest idea of the effect you have on men. It simply hasn't occurred to you that what I most want to do at this moment is carry you off to the nearest bed and make love to you for the rest of the afternoon—"

"You can't. I'm just one bruise from head to foot."

His eyes shone with an unholy glee. "Is that the only objection you're making?"

She blushed. "I have other things to do right now," she said primly.

"But you're not against the idea on principle?"

"No."

He touched her scarlet cheek with a gentle finger. "You're a darling, Ruth Gaynor. But you're right, we have other things to do right now. I've seen Miss Moir's will. It doesn't tell us much. She wrote you a private letter, which it mentions, that you should have had when you got your bequest."

"Yes, I read it. It didn't say much, only that I shouldn't allow myself to be tempted to give away the only inheritance I was ever likely to receive."

"Not a long letter?"

"Good heavens, no. A few words only. She said she hadn't been able to give me a refuge in her lifetime, so she was making up for it now, because it was her belief that every person should be independent, if possible. It was like her, you know. Looking back, I imagine she had a hard time getting her paintings accepted. I daresay Melissa Moir received many hard knocks and a great many patronizing reviews in her time, until the critics woke up and realized what they had in her."

"Did she tell you that in the letter?"

"She didn't have to. I work in the arts, too."

"Well, according to her will, some mention of her art should have been in the letter. Perhaps there were two letters. She got her first breaks in America and she left you instructions as to what to do with all her paintings, among other things. Her solicitor didn't give you such a letter?"

Ruth shook her head. "He was a very old man. Perhaps he forgot?"

"I doubt it. He probably didn't realize there were two letters. It didn't make much sense, but he probably didn't want to enquire too closely into the old lady's motives. Her family must have been restive even then."

"Then where is that other letter?"

"Somewhere in the cottage, I should think. Are you game to go back and look for it?"

Ruth clenched her fists, quite dreadfully afraid. "Do you really think it's necessary?"

"Well, it would help you decide what to do with the paintings. I don't think you'll actually find the letter. At a guess, I'd say it was lost when Miss Moir died, but Sylvia must have come to Lindisfarne to find it—that would account for the noises you've been hearing, and the missing key. It's also a strong possibility that she wanted to frighten you into selling the paintings. All I want you to do is to look for it, apparently alone, telling all and sundry that you know what it is you're looking for.''

"And do I?" Ruth asked.

"Oh yes. The old girl's solicitor—"

"Don't call her that!" Ruth interrupted him. "She was always Miss Moir. She even called me Miss Gaynor when I was only six years old."

He smiled at her with such affection that she could feel herself blushing again. "Miss Moir's solicitor kept copies of his correspondence with Miss Moir and I got a chance to read his files. I wish she had been allowed to bring you up because she recognized your quality even then. When she saw you again on the television, she decided she could trust you. She was afraid her family meant to murder her. All she wanted was to save her life's work from being sold off to finance that same family, who had never had a good word to say for her work. It took them a long time to find her. Then a few months ago, I suppose, Sylvia saw her obituary in the *Times*, mentioning Lindisfarne and stating, erroneously as it happens, that Miss Moir's paintings had been left to some trust or other. It took little time for her to find out that you had them and that, if anything happened to you, she could claim them, since she was Miss Moir's closest blood relative."

Ruth stared at him. "They wanted to kill her?" A terrible rage took possession of her. "They would have killed Miss Moir for a few paintings?"

"They would have killed her, my love, for several million dollars, but nature intervened. If she can, Sylvia will kill *you*, too."

The silence stretched into an eternity. Ruth's heart ached for her benefactor. How well she understood the loneliness Miss Moir must have known. And yet, loneliness didn't have to be Ruth's destiny as well. She had Aidan—at least, she thought she had. The breath caught in her throat. How did he know all this? Her old suspicions of him revived.

"You seem to have thought a great deal about it," she said. "What about Jonathan?"

"It's my idea that it was dark in the pub and Sylvia meant to kill you."

"How do you know?"

He gave her an angry look. "When you first told me about those noises in your cottage I began to think you were in danger. It didn't take me many enquiries to be sure of it! And I began figuring through things."

"I see," she said.

"No, you don't. I went to a lot of trouble to find out. Private detectives, friends in show business, you yourself! You don't know the hell I've been through, but it's been worth every minute. I knew I might lose you if I couldn't persuade you that I was the right man to trust—when you weren't even thinking in terms of any man. Don't you understand what you mean to me?"

Ruth stared at Aidan, making a discovery of her own. If their positions had been reversed, she would have felt exactly the same way. He needed her, but much more than that she needed him.

She held out a hand to Aidan. "I'll be safe, won't I, in Lindisfarne, while I search for that letter? Where will you be?" she said.

His eyes opaqued for a moment and Ruth saw that he was worried. Finally he said, "I think it's best that you don't know—you'll be safer that way. I have a plan. Judith will be with you, and I'll join you later. My love, do you trust me enough to leave it at that for now?''

Ruth looked away from him, feeling that the world itself would turn on her answer. Yes, the world, she thought. *Her* world—her future. Inside her something broke and it felt like the dawn. Ruth said, "Yes," smiling at Aidan with tears in her eyes. She heard him catch his breath.

He took her hand in his and kissed her palm, closing her fingers over the place as if to keep it safe. "I'll always be there for you, darling. Remember that."

Chapter Ten

Ellen Jenkins surveyed Ruth from head to foot. "Whatever have you been doing to yourself?"

Her mind on Aidan, Ruth stood fidgeting in her kitchen. She'd planned to invite her neighbour over and tell her of her impending search for the letter, but there had been no need. Mrs. Jenkins's radar for news was as acute as ever. She'd arrived at Ruth's back door on her own.

Ruth said, "I fell down some steps. Mrs. Jenkins—"

"Call me Ellen, dear. You're not Miss Moir and you never will be."

"Not Eileen? Sylvia Ross told me your name was Eileen."

"And what would she know about it? Never seen her more than a couple of times in my whole life. I hope she's not a friend of yours, my dear, because Miss Moir didn't like her. She never *said* anything, mind you, but I could tell. She shrank a couple of inches whenever that young woman came on the scene—or that husband of hers."

Ruth tried to put the shame of doubting Aidan away from her. "I wouldn't describe her as a friend," she said dryly. "I'd intended to call round and tell you I was here. I came up to look for a letter Miss Moir hid somewhere in the cottage. I didn't know about it before, but I think it will tell me what her wishes were concerning some of her things."

"I'd have thought you'd have that letter by now! Sure, I know about it. She put it in the wall safe she had installed in the bedroom. Want me to show you where it is?"

Ruth's spirits lifted. "If it isn't a bother to you. How many people know about it?"

"Well, my husband does. He put the safe in for her. Oh yes, she spent days writing you that letter. She didn't tell me what was in it, and I didn't ask her, mind you, but I know she had this idea about her paintings, some such nonsense about them being like fresh air, something that belongs to all of us. I daresay she didn't want them sold."

Ruth hid a smile. Ellen Jenkins was a typical country-woman, knowing far more than she was told about all her neighbours, almost by a process of osmosis. How much did she know about Ruth?

"If anything happens to me, what do you think would happen to the paintings?" she asked. Perhaps Ellen knew that, too.

"What should happen to you? You're young, you're healthy, aren't you? I daresay Miss Moir thought about all that before she put you in her will."

"I suppose so," she said. But had her "aunt" known that Ruth, too, would be in danger?

"It's a shame she couldn't trust that family of hers, really. Family is so important." Ellen went on. "I often thought Miss Moir could have starved for all those folk cared."

"I suppose they despised her success," Ruth said, "more than they despised her."

"Aye, jealousy does that to people. Ah well, who are we to judge them, dearie? Miss Moir wasn't the sharing sort, either. You have to learn to love if you want to be loved." Ruth looked askance at the friendly, blustery woman and was glad she didn't know the worst of what Miss Moir's family had done.

Ellen stayed for a cup of tea after she had shown Ruth the safe in the bedroom wall. Ruth was only mildly surprised when the other woman rattled off the combination and opened it for her.

"Nothing in it!" Ellen had exclaimed as the door swung open.

"Perhaps she put the letter somewhere else," Ruth suggested now, still disappointed.

"Must have done," said Ellen, finishing off her tea. "It's mighty strange that she should have done that, though, don't you think? Are you sure her lawyer didn't have it?"

"No, I think it's here somewhere," Ruth said, with more cheer than she felt.

Judith, having been napping after the drive and awakening at the sound of voices, waited for several moments after Ellen had gone before going downstairs. "The village gossip?" she asked Ruth with lifted brows.

"A *caring* neighbour! She was the only friend Miss Moir had," Ruth chided.

Judith turned away from Ruth's hurt expression. "That doesn't have to be your future, too, if that's what you're thinking," she said awkwardly.

"I know," said Ruth firmly, and she realized she did. "Aidan told me about your husband. I'm sorry."

Judith summoned up a smile. "I'll survive. I may even marry again—if I'm not having too much fun managing your future."

"That's what I want to talk to you about," Ruth blurted out, hoping Judith wouldn't be too upset by what she was about to say. "I'll always want to work, but I think I ought to warn you that it won't be quite the same." She could have said that being away from Aidan, even for a few days, was proving to be a traumatic experience. Why had she even agreed to leave him behind in London? Suppose something should happen to *him*?

"Other fish to fry?"

"Maybe. I want to pick and choose what I do—and have more time off. Is that possible?"

Judith nodded decisively. "I'll see what I can do."

It was the following day, before they heard anything from Aidan. Judith had taken herself off for a walk before the rain really set in for the day.

Ruth watched her departure, shaking her head with exasperation at the gloomy weather. She had wanted her friend to see Lindisfarne at its very best, with a pride that had startled her. For years she had thought of London as being her home, with Lindisfarne no more than a distant memory of childhood. Now, it was London that had lost its pull on Ruth. She wanted little more than to live on Lindisfarne with Aidan forever and ever. How she hoped he was still safe.

She prayed it would be Aidan as soon as the telephone rang.

It was! "Where are you?" she asked.

Ruth relaxed. She could hear the reassuring laughter in his voice as he answered. "I'm at Gatwick Airport. I'm flying up to Durham and I should be with you for dinner. How's Judith?"

"Bored by our country ways."

"*Our* country ways?"

Ruth pursed her lips and changed the subject. That was the trouble with lawyers, she decided, they were too acute to the slightest nuance of voice. She wanted to tell him face to face how she felt about London—and about him!

"I've missed you."

His voice was dark and dropped at least an octave. "Hold on up there," he said, "I'm coming."

Judith came home looking like a drowned rat. Her high heels were hopelessly caked with mud. In answer to her mute look of enquiry, Ruth grinned, but suppressed her laughter.

"You've heard from Aidan!" Judith nearly shouted.

"How did you guess?"

Judith rushed to Ruth and hugged her happily. "Actresses don't fool me, darling. You can try to look as nonchalant as you please, but you still look worlds better than you did when I left here to explore the place of your birth. How soon can I go back to London?"

"Bad as that?" Ruth laughed.

"I'm not the outdoor type."

Ruth hugged herself, smiling. "He's flying up to Durham. He'll be here sometime this evening."

"Is that all he said?" Judith drawled.

"More or less," Ruth said dreamily.

Aidan's arrival was delayed by the tide. It was only with difficulty that Ruth restrained herself from driving out to watch it subside, inch by inch.

"I guess we could search for the letter now," she suggested to Judith.

Judith raised her eyebrows. "*You* may search for the letter! I'm going to huddle over the fire and dream of my beautiful central heating at home. Tell me, did Aidan sound cheerful when he rang?"

"Very." But Ruth was pacing around the room.

"Good. It sounds as if Aidan is just fine. Stop worrying about him, will you? He'll tell us all about it when he gets here."

Ruth had walked all the way to the end of the causeway before she realized she had made up her mind to meet him. The rain had stopped and a rainbow rose over the mainland in an arc so beautiful that she caught her breath. There was nothing like that to be seen in London.

She knew it was Aidan long before she heard the swish of his tyres in the outgoing tide. He came to a stop within inches of where she was standing and opened the passenger door for her to get in beside him.

"Darling," he greeted her. "I had to wait for a half hour before I dared come over the causeway—the longest half hour of my life!"

Her glance met his squarely. "Tell me about it," she invited him. "But I think I should tell you that I'm not some helpless female, ready to fall into your gallant arms," she joked. "Far from it! Suppose you dismount from your snow-white charger and try consulting me for a change?"

The tired lines in his face brought her to a jarring stop. With gentle fingers, she rubbed the line of his jaw, wondering why a man who needed a shave should still manage to look so sexy to her. He put an arm round her shoulders and drew her close to him. She kissed him gravely on the cheek. "Suppose you tell me all about it," she suggested.

From the back door, Ruth could see all the way to Cuddie's Island. It was calming to stand there, leaning against the portal and staring into the distance. There was something special about Lindisfarne. Perhaps it was that St. Cuthbert, some thirteen hundred years before the Nature Conservancy had caught up with him, expressed his love for all God's creatures by turning the whole of Lindisfarne into an animal sanctuary of sorts. The place bred love and tolerance and a oneness with all things.

"Am I forgiven?" Aidan asked from behind her.

Ruth made an impatient sound. "It's got nothing to do with forgiveness. It's got to do with the way we relate to each other. I want to have my say in what happens to me."

Aidan's mouth tightened. "You'd been hurt enough," he said gently. "I wasn't going to stand by and let Sylvia have another go at you."

"Wasn't that my choice?" She turned to him.

"Well, I suppose I have a father complex where you're concerned."

Ruth hunched her shoulders. "You're not going to put me in the wrong about this, Aidan. I had a right to know what was going on. I was so worried about you."

He ran a hand through his hair and her heart went out to him.

"Okay, so you had a right to know. But haven't I the right to spare you more pain and disillusionment. Ruth, I don't think you know what I went through when I lifted you off the pavement and took you to the hospital."

She moved closer to him, her eyes soft and warm with love. "I'm glad you're safe. Now, tell me what happened with Sylvia." She hesitated, then closed the gap between them. "I do understand, but I'm all grown-up, Aidan, and grown-up people have to meet on equal terms, or—or it doesn't work."

For an instant he looked very much the lawyer he was. He braced himself to take most of her weight, his legs a little apart, and his eyes bright beneath frowning brows as he put his arms around her.

"You've made your point. If I promise never to decide what's best for you without proper consultation ever again, may we kiss and make up?"

Ruth nodded, suddenly breathless. "I want that very much," she whispered.

Aidan's kiss was warm and gentle and she never wanted it to end. It was he who broke away first, a subtle air of triumph about him. She might have made her point, she thought ruefully, but he had certainly trumped her ace. Once in his arms, she couldn't care less what Sylvia had been up to.

"Judith and I looked everywhere, but we didn't find the letter," she told him.

"It'll turn up," he answered with unexpected certainty. "This is how it went. By passing a rumor to a producer—an 'angel' friend of mine, I gave Sylvia to believe that you had already found the letter and had left it in my care at my flat—"

"Did she come looking for it?" Ruth's eyes opened wide.

"She did. She hadn't found it up here, so she was bound to take the bait sooner or later. If she was to walk away with the paintings, she had to destroy that letter, and she knew it."

Ruth bit her lip. "Was it horrible when she showed up?"

"It was, rather," he admitted. "No violence, but there's something terrible about naked greed, to my mind. The police were glad to assist me. A single-minded lady, that. They agreed with my idea that Sylvia must have meant to kill you in the pub."

"I know. I kept telling myself that she didn't mean to kill Jon. That *had* to be an accident, didn't it?"

"He deserved it, but I suppose we'll never know. Better not to," Aidan observed.

Ruth shuddered. Some of her misery showed on her face. "Poor Miss Moir! I hope I prove worthy of her trust. No one person should own those paintings..." Ruth's gaze swept up to Aidan's eyes. "We do such dreadful things to one another, don't we? One failure in love leads to another. Miss Moir's family failed. Miss Moir failed. I wish I could show her the loving care she missed when she was alive."

"Very profound, Miss Gaynor. I bet that's exactly what she wished about you."

Her eyes clouded. "I could have become another Miss Moir. I'm lucky I found you first."

His arms went around her. Ruth could feel him tremble with rage as he thought about what she had gone through. Could anyone care about her so much? She knew he wanted her physically, that he loved her, but it gave her an intensely warm feeling to know that he hurt when she hurt, that his instinct was to protect her—even if she couldn't always approve of his methods. There was more to this loving business than she had ever realized.

"I love you," Ruth said.

Aidan pressed her to him. "Marry me, Ruth," he murmured. "Marry me, here, on Lindisfarne, before anything else happens to you. I understand how much your independence means to you, but I wouldn't be much of a man if I didn't want to do all I can to protect you, to keep you safe. *Hinny*, I love you."

Ruth rubbed a finger against the roughness of his beard, learning that in some ways he was as vulnerable as she. "Dear heart, I've been basking in your love every since you fed me baked beans and said you wanted to wring my neck. Nothing seems as bad as it did when I was on my own—even when you're not there, I can feel you beside me, loving me. All I'm asking is that we do things together."

For a moment Aidan looked as if he couldn't believe his ears. "You'll marry me?"

"As soon as possible!"

He let out a whoop of joy. "Special licence? I'll have to let my parents know. Judith will stay on?"

Ruth considered. "I hope so. Do you think I ought to ask her to 'give me away'? She'll look on it like that anyway, if I give up my career."

Aidan went quite pale. "Is that what you think I want? Oh, no. Of course you're going on with your career!"

Ruth's brow creased in confusion. "But I want children. Lots of your children who'll all be company for one another."

Aidan began to laugh. "Can't we have a bit of everything?" he asked her.

She gave him a quick, uncertain glance. Was that what he really wanted? It was what *she* wanted, of course, but there was such a thing as being too greedy in this life.

"I can see I'm going to be spoilt rotten!" she sighed.

Aidan's smile was contented, and his kiss was very gentle. "It's about time someone had the fun of spoiling you," he said.

The wedding wasn't quite as either of them had expected. The people of Lindisfarne had remembered that Ruth Gaynor was one of their own and, led by Ellen Jenkins, they threw themselves into the celebration with a will. Everyone provided something toward the feast, shyly presenting their produce from the sea or their baking as if it were the most natural thing in the world to do so. The only difficulty was finding space enough for them all to crowd into Ruth's tiny cottage after the brief ceremony in the small, ancient church, redolent with the atmosphere of the old Celtic saints.

It had been an exhausting few days for Ruth. While Aidan disappeared to Durham to tell his parents the good news about the marriage and to arrange for them to drive to Lindisfarne on the morning of the wedding, she had searched every inch of the cottage for Miss Moir's letter. On the second day she had found it—after she'd almost given up the hunt—in the drawer of her dressing table. With trembling hands, Ruth had opened the envelope, giving an excited call to Judith, who came running. "Here, let me see!" Judith had cried. She snatched the paper from Ruth's hand and began to read aloud:

Dear Miss Gaynor,

How pleasant it is to see you have grown up to be just the sort of person I hoped you would be. You're a fine actress, of course, but you will never make the kind of villainess I recently saw you trying to portray. I have experience of such persons; you obviously have none. Once they have you cornered, they no longer bother to be charming to your face, let alone behind your back.

But to business. I fear I am not very much longer for this world. Please don't think I mind, I don't. What I do care about is the fate of my paintings. They are dearer to me than any progeny. This is why I am leaving them to you. They may not be to your personal taste, but accept my word that one day they will be considered some of the best watercolours my generation has produced in this country.

I don't want my work hidden away. Nor do I want it to be exhibited in London, or America, where no one knows me. Lindisfarne gave me refuge at a time when I needed it, and it is here I should like my work to be on permanent display. Do what you can to make this dream of mine come true, but not if it involves any risk to your own life.

If, in three years, you are unable to find a civic home you can approve of for my paintings, they are to become your own and you must deal with them in any way you think fit. I trust you, Ruth Gaynor, as I cannot trust my own family, and I wish we had had more time together before you were taken from me. Forgive a lonely, old woman for taking up so much of your time. I hope that you learn from the mistakes I have made. Other people may be hell, but they are also heaven—a fact I learned far too late in life.

God bless you,
Melissa Moir

Miss Moir's letter moved Ruth to act. Judith had been a silent spectator after they'd read the missive, refusing to help Ruth tackle the local civic bodies with a view to set up a single gallery, where all Melissa Moir's paintings could be shown together. Keen as the townspeople were to have such a thing within Lindisfarne's boundaries, the cuts in local funds and the cost of insuring such a collection gave them pause.

"Miss Moir didn't want her paintings to go to London!" Ruth said again and again. "She was a *northern* artist! There must be some way of keeping her work up here as she wanted."

In the end, a determined councillor had taken Ruth aside. "Look, Miss Gaynor, the best thing you can do is sell a couple of the paintings and set up a gallery yourself. Why don't you put it in trust for the people of Lindisfarne? I reckon Miss Moir would have liked that. There's nothing that I can see to stop you from taking the whole thing into your own hands."

Ruth decided to take his advice. It hadn't been difficult to enthuse the local community with Mrs. Jenkins's help. They agreed together on which of her paintings to sell, deciding to send them to America, because Miss Moir had first won recognition there. For the rest of the watercolours, they had formed a trust and, with the help of the bank and the insurance company, they had made the first step to open a Melissa Moir gallery on Lindisfarne.

"Likely as not, you'll be here to see how it goes?" Mrs. Jenkins had said to Ruth.

"As often as I can," she had assured her.

"That young man of yours will have something to say about that," had been the reply.

"He can always come with me," she answered, eyes twinkling.

"Aye, he's made himself as much at home here as if he were one of us! It'll suit him better when he doesn't have to room at my house, though, I'll be bound! He's a good lad, that one! You couldn't do no better for yourself, Ruth Gaynor. Miss Moir would've been pleased to see you settled. Imagine that family of hers.

Ruth shook her head. She didn't want to remember Sylvia Ross and what was happening to her now. She was relieved that her own fate would have little more to do with her from now on. She would have to give evidence at the trial, as Aidan had explained to her, but she would have his support through that ordeal. She preferred to think about how Miss Moir would have given her approval to the man she had chosen to be her life's companion.

The day of the wedding dawned clear and bright. Once inside the church, Ruth forgot all else but Aidan. She, whose whole life had been working an audience, forgot that there was anyone else there. She might have been completely alone as she walked down the aisle toward him, smiling a secret smile as she finally took her position by his side. She was as glad as Pollyanna! That's what falling in love with him had done for her, she reflected. Who cared what anyone else thought of how she was, or the way she spoke her vows, or the skip of joy with which she turned from signing the register and took his arm to walk between the whole assembled community and out into the sunshine of their future life together?

It was a reversal of the usual procedure when the bride and groom stood on the doorstep and waved the last of the reception guests away. Judith was spending the night with Aidan's parents in Durham before travelling back to London. Everyone else had their own homes to go to, or had made arrangements to slip away to the mainland at low tide—always a feature of life on the island.

Alone at last, Ruth fell into her husband's arms. "Hasn't it been a lovely day?" she murmured.

"I hope that isn't a preamble to warn me you're too tired for what's to come?"

She chuckled. It was a warm, delightful sound, quite different from the shyness he would expect from a virgin on her wedding night. "That," she said, "is going to be the perfect end to a perfect day."

His silence made her look up at him. "Having doubts?" she asked him with a light naughtiness that caught at his heartstrings.

"It may not be perfect for you the first time," he warned her.

But she had no doubts whatsoever. "I shall be with you," she said simply. She ran the bath. Getting in, she swirled the scented water with her flannel and began to scrub herself with it. Then, quite suddenly, Aidan was in the bathroom with her.

"Want me to do your back for you?" he grinned at her.

She was beyond speech. He was as naked as she was herself and she couldn't tear her eyes away from him. She struggled for the carefree confidence that had been hers all day.

"You're beautiful," she said at last. And he was! Why on earth were painted nudes almost invariably female? It was incomprehensible to her.

"You're beautiful, too," he said huskily. And certainly he seemed to find her so. He took her flannel from her and washed her back with fierce concentration. Then he started on the rest of her. Her eyes met his.

"Please, take me to bed," she whispered.

"Don't you want me to dry you first?"

She shook her head, her urgency increased. She took her flannel out of his hand, giving him her hand in exchange. The washcloth fell, unnoticed, into the water. Ruth pulled herself to her feet and stepped out of the bath, her knees weak. Then, sweeping her off her feet, Aidan carried her across the landing and into the bedroom.

"You must have known an awful lot of women in your time," she said without resentment.

His fingers stroked the soft curves of her breasts. "Rehearsals, merely," he said.

Shared laughter made a pleasant aftermath to shared passion, Ruth discovered. "It's a good thing I'm a quick study!"

"Isn't it just!" he agreed. "How about another performance?"

"Oh, break a leg!" she said.

Ruth slept late the next morning. Aidan brought her a cup of coffee when he could wait for her no longer. For a long moment, he stood looking down at her as she slept, and wondered that someone so shy, so reticent, should have come to life in such a blaze of passion in his arms. He pulled on the sheet with which she had cocooned herself. She stirred like a contented kitten and smiled up at him.

"Coffee!" she exclaimed with satisfaction. "I was lonely without you," she added. "Why didn't you wait?"

"You were asleep," Aidan said.

Ruth nodded, still smiling. "It was a long, sleepless night, and I was just catching up. I knew when you got out of bed, though." She took a sip of coffee, placing the cup on the bedside table with a joyous movement. "Aren't you going to kiss me good-morning?"

"It depends if you want any breakfast or not?"

She thought about it. He had always thought her eyes to be her best feature, but with the slow-burning fire of passion in their depths, he found himself hoping no other man would ever see her in quite this mood.

"You're already dressed," she said at last.

"A mistake," he admitted. "I didn't realize one didn't dress for one's honeymoon."

"No, of course not," Ruth exclaimed. "This is a first for you, too, isn't it?" She rose from the bed, turning to grin at him over her shoulder. "I'm going to choose breakfast. Bad luck!"

His eyes flickered over her. "I didn't hurt you last night, did I?"

She went to him at once. "No, my love, you opened the gates of paradise for me. I thought you knew that."

"Then what's so attractive about breakfast?" he demanded.

"I'm hungry!"

He sighed. "All right, breakfast," he conceded. "Then we'll make love again!"

Ruth was still laughing at him when she came out of the bathroom and sat down before her dressing table to fix her hair. She felt alive and absolutely wonderful. Looking at herself in the glass, she had a glimpse of the fleeting beauty that others saw in her. She felt incredibly happy; she wanted to be beautiful for Aidan.

Aidan had said he wanted to spoil her and he was doing his best to do so as he placed her breakfast in front of her. "I'm getting lazy already," Ruth said.

"That's all right with me," he replied and smiled at her.

"I love you."

"I should certainly hope so," Aidan retorted. "You married me, didn't you?"

She didn't mind his teasing. "Best thing I ever did!" Ruth said.

The post arrived through the door with a dull plop. Ruth was on her feet at once, hurrying into the hall to retrieve it. She saw at once that the large buff envelope held the manuscript of a play, so it came as no surprise to her to see her married name and address written in Judith's distinctive hand on the front.

She tore it open, going slowly back into the kitchen.

"Anything interesting?" Aidan asked her.

"Work." She read the brief note, explaining that Judith hadn't liked to interrupt her wedding day with talk of future events, but that she felt herself that this play was exactly the opportunity Ruth had been waiting for.

Aidan recognized the signs as he watched her flip through the typescript, her fingers trembling with suppressed excitement. He felt exactly the same way when a particularly fascinating brief crossed his desk. "Exciting stuff?"

Ruth took a deep breath. She mentioned the name of the playwright in a hushed whisper. "This has to be the role of my dreams!"

Immediately she felt guilty. She put the script down on the table, determined to forget all about it. No one could have everything, and it had been only the day before that she had chosen to be Aidan's wife!

"Aren't you going to read it?"

She cast him a swift look from below her lashes. "I don't think right now is quite the time, do you?" she said coolly.

He picked up the play and handed it to her, pulling her close to him.

"I think now is exactly the right time. You want to do it, don't you?"

Silently, she nodded her head.

"I want you to do it, too. I'm as much in love with Ruth Gaynor as I am with Mrs. Aidan Wakefield, you know. I don't want to see her neglected. I'm pretty proud of her, if you want to know!"

Ruth put her head on his shoulder, hugging him hard. "I must have done something wonderful to be married to you! Darling, I love you so much it hurts!"

He kissed her cheek and then her lips. "Now that is something I intend to do something about—*immediately*!" he promised her.

*   *   *   *   *

COMING NEXT MONTH

#580 CALHOUN—Diana Palmer
Calhoun Ballenger had raised Abby Clark since childhood, but now
that she was twenty-one, she'd set his heart on fire...and was
determined to make this long, tall Texan her own! The first book of
Diana Palmer's LONG, TALL TEXANS trilogy!

#581 THE SCORPIO MAN—Sara Grant
Melissa Wyatt came to Elba for underwater photography—not for a
romance with some mysterious playboy. So what if Nico Giordano's
eyes were as green and deep as the sea? She wasn't about to be stung
by a Scorpio man.

#582 WORDS OF LOVE—Octavia Street
Was devastatingly attractive Christopher Fields a spy, a gunrunner or
a Secret Service man? Annie White didn't know, but there was no
defense against his words of love....

#583 AN INDEPENDENT LADY—Roslyn McDonald
Dirk Warner had hired aloof architect Terry Lovell to restore his
antebellum house, but suddenly he had plans of his own to make a
house into a home. Would his love restore Terry's broken heart?

#584 RAINDANCE AUTUMN—Phyllis Halldorson
Reserved Annelise Kelsey was looking for love with a city slicker.
Could a rugged country man like Rusty Watt convince her he was just
the shining knight she'd been waiting for?

#585 MOON IN THE WATER—Victoria Glenn
Jacob Van Cleef wouldn't tolerate anyone challenging his authority
over the small town of Half Moon Falls—until fiery Liza Langley
breezed into town and poked her pretty nose into his business....

AVAILABLE THIS MONTH:

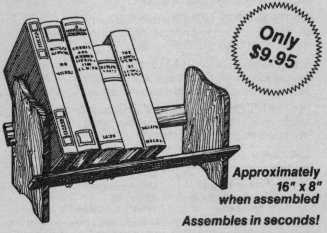